Hunt

for

Hollowdeep

Dedication

David:
Levi and Liza

Charlie:
Jim
From cars to guitars, thanks for everything.

Special thanks from the co-authors to Steven Spenser
Ledford for bringing Knightscares to life with his vivid
imagination and careful eye for detail.

ISBN 0-9728461-5-8

Printed in the U.S.A.

Second Printing, January 2008

Hunt for Hollowdeep
Table of Contents

Fantasy Name Guide for Hunt for Hollowdeep

In fantasy books like Knightscares, some character names will be familiar to you. Some will not. To help you pronounce the tough ones, here's a handy guide to the unusual names found in *Hunt for Hollowdeep*.

Agamemnon
Agg - uh - mem - non

Efreet
Eh - freet

Jasiah
Jay - sigh - uh

Naglamound
Nag - luh - mound

Shaddim
Shah - dim (dim as in a light, not deem)

Shelolth
She - lolth

Sludgemite
Sludge - might

Virgil VonWinchester
Vur - jull   Von - Win -chess - ter

Wyvern
Why - vern

Hollowdeep

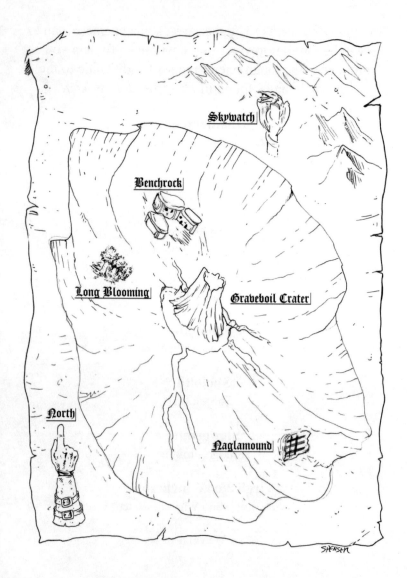

Tiller's Field and Surroundings

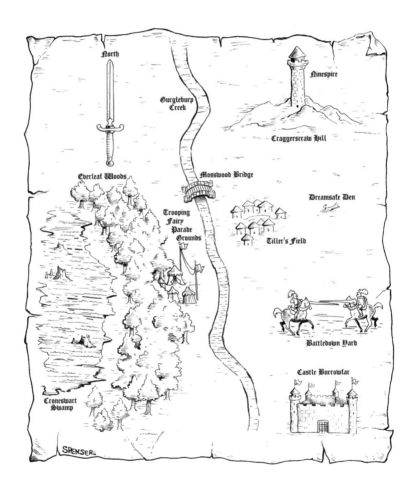

North

Gurgleburp Creek

Ninespire

Craggerscraw Hill

Everleaf Woods

Mosswood Bridge

Dreamsafe Den

Trooping Fairy Parade Grounds

Tiller's Field

Battledown Yard

Castle Burrowlar

Croneswart Swamp

SPENSER

Legend of the Dragonsbane Horn

One waits with the wizard
In his hollow tome.
One sounds in the sands
Of the dwarven home.
One rings wrapped in roots
In damp forest loam.
One drones in the dark
Where the shaddim roam.

Four for the future.
Four 'fore the reign.
Four for the forging.
Of Horn Dragonsbane.

Knightscares #6:
Hunt for Hollowdeep

David Anthony
and
Charles David

Tunnel Vision

1

I dreamed of fire in underground tunnels. Blazing pillars erupted from the floor and bathed the walls in bloody red. Smoke stung my eyes. Fumes choked my breath. I screamed without making a sound.

Laughter filled my dream, too. Taunting, hateful laughter. It hissed in every corner and flame, always ahead of me, behind, and close. Hearing it reminded me of a red-faced bully.

I started to run. My skin dripped with sweat and my vision blurred. Waves of heat rippled and danced in the air.

Racing wildly around a corner, I spotted it—the Dragonsbane Horn. The magical instrument hung in the air, rotating slowly over a cauldron of simmering lava.

That's why I'm here, I realized. *The Horn needs me.* I wasn't named Jasiah Dragonsbane for nothing. Protecting the Horn was part of what I'd been born to do.

But the Horn didn't look quite the way I expected. This Horn was whole. It had four pieces connected together end-to-end. My Horn—the *real* Horn—only had three pieces. The fourth was lost, and it was my job to find it.

That told me this dream wasn't about the present. It was a vision of the past or the future.

I reached timidly for the Horn with my right hand. Even in a dream, I wasn't surprised to find that I wore my gauntlet. It had become a part of me.

The gauntlet was a thick leather glove that reached almost to my elbow. A number of buckles and straps kept it in place, and deep scratches covered its surface.

It was a sign of who I was and more. My Uncle Arick had given it to me but hadn't told me why. I'd had to figure that out myself. One of the first things I'd learned was that I couldn't take it off no matter how hard I tried. The gauntlet's magic stopped me whenever I tried.

My fingers brushed the Horn, causing it to spin faster. It bobbed out of reach like a cork bobbing on water.

"Come … here," I grunted, standing on my tiptoes and stretching for all I was worth.

Glurp!

The lava in the cauldron suddenly belched, and I snatched my arm back.

Glurp, gloop-gloop, glurp!

Hiccupping bubbles swelled and popped. Sizzling droplets splattered my tunic. Something was rising up from the lava.

A flame-red shape slowly took form. First a jelly-like ooze, the shape solidified as it continued to rise. Five fingers appeared then a hand and arm. Straps and buckles coiled about its length.

The lava was imitating my gauntlet!

The lava-gauntlet's fingers spread and grasped the Dragonsbane Horn. A flash of orange light pulsed, and the fresh scent of something burning clogged the air.

I yelped in horror. The Horn was melting, and I had to save it.

This time I leaped, both hands clutching after the Horn. The lava-gauntlet was pulling it down, down into the cauldron. If that happened, the Horn would be lost forever.

My hands found their mark, but I shrieked and let go instantly. *Such pain!* Awful heat burned into my skin and seared my bones. The agony of it drove me to my knees.

Through tears, I gazed up as the Horn slipped away. The lava dragged it into the cauldron, bubbled once more, then went still. A deep red splotch pooled at the surface like blood rising from a wound.

I hung my head, tears still streaming from my eyes. One thought echoed hauntingly in my mind.

I've destroyed the Dragonsbane Horn.

Laughter howled through the tunnels and the flames danced higher.

Midnight Crack

2

I came awake gasping for air. My blanket lay kicked on the floor, and I was sweating. My palms and fingers tingled painfully.

The Horn! I panicked, stabbing a hand beneath my pillow. If anything had happened …

Toongk.

My fingers collided with something solid, and I sighed with relief. The Horn was unharmed and exactly where I'd left it. Too bad I couldn't say the same about my tender hand.

I rolled over, hoping to fall back to sleep. Darkness outside the window told me it was too early to be morning. There was no reason to be awake.

But my mind had other ideas. It replayed my dream, demanding answers. Had the dream been a glimpse of the future? Had it been some kind of warning?

Normally I don't pay attention to dreams. They're mostly meaningless, not predictions of the future. The only thing more boring than trying to figure out my own dreams was to hear about someone else's.

But this dream was different. It had a feeling of magic about it. A feeling of doom. It told me I would destroy the Dragonsbane Horn.

But why would I do that? I'd spent so much time trying to find it and keep it safe. A lot of people had. I couldn't imagine harming the Horn.

Long ago, the Horn had been broken into four pieces. Wizard Ast had given me the first piece. My friends and I had rescued the next two from monsters. The fourth was still missing, but I thought I knew who had it.

Shelolth.

Shelolth was a horrible black dragon who wanted the Horn. She hunted its pieces and me. She'd even created a terrifying army of ghost-like monsters called shaddim to help her.

If anyone had the last piece, it was Shelolth. I didn't need a nightmare to tell me that. My quest wouldn't end until I faced her.

—You will not face her alone, Jasiah Dragonsbane—a metallic female voice whispered reassuringly in my mind.

The voice belonged to Talon, my guardian and best friend. Talon was a wyvern, a creature similar to a dragon but small enough to perch on my gauntlet like a falcon. She had amazingly colorful feathers and scales, and could speak to me and hear what I said over great distances. She could also read my mind.

"Eavesdropping again?" I joked. I was glad to know she'd be with me when I faced Shelolth, but I wasn't going to come right out and say that. It was more fun to tease her. "Don't you ever sleep?"

Talon's reply came immediately. —Don't you?—

Like I said, I liked to tease Talon, and she teased right back. I'm just not sure if I ever got the best of her.

"I'm going to check on the egg," I said to change the subject. Talon had won that round.

—In the middle of the night? It could be dangerous.— By dangerous, she meant there could be shaddim, Shelolth's ghosts. They came out in dark places, especially at night.

I shrugged even though Talon couldn't see me. "I can't sleep. Besides, with you around, what do I have to be afraid of?"

Talon didn't respond, and I thought I might have actually won a round. If she argued, what would that say about her ability to protect me?

I smiled at that. Talon one, Jasiah one. It was a whole new game.

I cleaned up and dressed quietly. My Uncle Arick slept in the next bed, and I didn't want to wake him. He was as big as a bear and would be as grouchy as one if he knew where I was going.

That wasn't to say Uncle Arick was mean. He was protective. He was also the biggest, strongest, and bravest man I'd ever met. People from all around called him a hero, including me.

Unfortunately, big and strong ran out in my family after Uncle Arick. Who knew about brave? I'm so short and small that most strangers think I'm nine years old. That would be fine if I weren't eleven and a half!

But what I've learned on my quest for the Horn is that heroes come in all varieties. Looks, talent, background, gender—these things don't make heroes. Regular people make heroes through heart and hard work.

I slipped silently out the window. My uncle and I were guests in Sheriff Logan's home. It wouldn't be polite to wake the sheriff in the middle of the night.

On top of that, it wouldn't do me any good to wake anyone. If I did, I'd be sent to bed without seeing the egg.

My friend Connor had found the egg while helping me search for the third piece of the Horn. It was an unhatched dragon egg. Only it wouldn't stay unhatched for long. A long crack had recently appeared down its center.

No one in Tiller's Field wanted the egg in their house, so Sheriff Logan let us store it in his shed. I guess the thought of waking up to a baby dragon at the foot of the bed seemed like a bad idea. It would sure give new meaning to

the expression *the early bird gets the wyrm! Wyrm* is a
word for dragon that sounds just like *worm*.

I tiptoed across the backyard. The sky was cloudy, and I
couldn't see the moon or stars. Lucky for me my eyes and
ears are as good as a cat's, even at night.

Vrrr-errr-nnnt.

The door to the shed creaked as it opened, and the
sudden noise set my heart to racing. Why was I breathing
so hard?

The first thing I noticed inside the shed was all the
weapons. Spears, swords, bows, maces, and dangerous-
looking things I couldn't name hung from the walls. Sheriff Logan obviously didn't have yard work in mind. There
wasn't a single rake or wheelbarrow.

Soft red light filled the shed, casting bloody shadows on
the weapons. I was starting to have second thoughts.
Maybe this wasn't the best place to visit in the middle of
the night.

K-k-k-krrreck!

A scratchy cracking sound grabbed my attention. The
egg was hatching!

As tall as the space between the floor and a door handle,
the egg stood balanced on its larger rounded end in one
corner. Red and black swirls painted its surface. We had
wrapped blankets around it to keep it warm.

K-k-k-krrreck!

The egg trembled and cracked again. Bits of dark shell popped free.

I took a cautious step back. Suddenly, I didn't want to be near the egg. When the dragon hatched, wouldn't it be hungry? A hatched dragon wouldn't behave like a newborn puppy!

—Get out!— Talon's voice was almost a shriek in my mind.

I wanted to flee, but my eyes were glued to the egg.

K-k-k-KRRRECK! The crack down its center split wide.

A Bad Yoke

3

The egg throbbed wetly, pumping like a laboring heart. Red light swelled and dimmed with every pulse.

I shouldn't be here, I told myself, wishing Uncle Arick would show up to send me back to bed. But I still couldn't tear my eyes away. The egg was fascinating, and I took a step closer.

K-k-k-krrreck!

Fragments of shell split and peeled like old paint. Cracks on the egg's surface formed a spiderweb design.

Every step I took seemed to excite the egg. The closer I got, the faster it hatched. When I froze with my foot in the air, the egg went still.

"What's going on here?" I whispered. I wasn't tapping the egg with a spoon or looking to make breakfast. It should hatch when it was ready, not because of me.

I lowered my foot and the egg wobbled, reminding me of an impatient person tapping a foot. *K-k-k-krrreck!*

That did it. The egg was watching me, or listening.

Somehow it knew what I was doing.

Without turning, I reached behind me for the door. I hoped the egg would forget about me if I moved as slowly as possible. My fingers brushed against something metal and—

Clar-rrrrang!

A tangle of Sheriff Logan's weapons clattered to the floor. I gave a start and the egg burst. So much for sneaking.

Glook!

Chunky black fluid like rotten egg yoke spewed into the air. It splattered sickeningly on the walls and floor, soaking my boots. What an awful smell!

—Beware! Flee!— Talon cried.

"Where are you?" I shot back. She should have been here already.

Looking to take her advice, I spun toward the door. If I didn't run now, I wouldn't get another chance. Something hideous was hatching from the egg.

My boots slipped in the syrupy ooze, and I went down hard. Sticky wetness drenched my clothing and scalded my skin.

"Hurry, Talon!" I called, lying on my back. This nightmare was too much. The darkness, the slime, the stink—I needed help.

I groped with my gauntlet for anything I could find and

came up clutching the handle of a bucket. Of all the luck! In a shed stocked with weapons, I managed to grab something used to carry slop to the pigs. How typically Jasiah!

Glook! Glook!

All around me, lumpy black bodies as big as my feet wiggled and crawled from the stinking sludge. Some had dozens of twitching, spider-like legs. Others slithered on their bellies like slugs. All of them looked unfinished and deformed, like lumps of wet clay cast aside by a sculptor.

—Don't let them touch you!— Talon squawked in warning. —Sludgemites are as dangerous as shaddim.—

Sludgemites?

I gasped and kicked my feet, scooting on my backside away from the filthy beasts. If they were as bad as shaddim, I was in more trouble than I'd realized. One touch from a shaddim would put a victim to sleep.

How was I going to keep hundreds of sludgemites from crawling all over me?

23

Swarm Storm

4

Glook! Glook!

Sludgemites scuttled everywhere. Their crooked legs clicked on the floorboards, walls, and ceiling. Their moist wings sprayed strands of slime. I felt like I'd stumbled into a nest of sneezing spiders.

"Anytime now, Talon!" I bellowed, clawing my way to my feet, the useless bucket still clutched in my fist. Fear has a way of getting people moving fast.

—Do you think I'm enjoying a midnight snack?— the wyvern huffed. —I'm up to my tail feathers in sludgemites out here.—

For now, at least, I'd have to save myself. Talon was doing her best, and I was on my own.

The bucket was surprisingly heavy. As I charged out of the shed, water sloshed from it.

Water! I should have known. Sheriff Logan had wisely placed a bucket of water close by in case the hatched dragon the we'd all thought would hatch got out of hand.

Too bad it hadn't been a dragon that had hatched. It would have been a whole lot easier to manage one baby dragon than a nest of squirming sludgemites. There's a big difference between something trying to eat you because it's hungry and because it's just plain mean.

Outside the shed wasn't any better than inside. Sludgemites swarmed the air in thick clouds and blanketed the ground like creeping carpets. Globs of slime glistened in the grass. I almost ran back inside and slammed the door.

In the middle of it all, Talon looped and spun like a trapeze artist. Her jeweled eyes flashed and her long tail slashed like a whip.

A sludgemite zipped in close, spattering my cheek with slime. I threw myself to the left and somehow managed to not spill a drop from the bucket. Why was I still carrying the dumb thing?

"Do you have a plan?" I shouted at Talon.

Sludgemites continued to slink and slither from the shed. There had to be at least one of them for every person in town. That was one big egg!

—Blow the Horn— Talon said firmly, but I barely heard her. I was thinking of something else.

One of them for every person. The words repeated in my mind, and a shiver chilled my spine. Was the number of sludgemites a coincidence? Or could it be related to the number of townsfolk?

The chill in my spine iced over. The sleep-touch of a sludgemite turned victims into shaddim. That's what happened to those who didn't wake. It was like getting bitten on the neck by a vampire.

That was Shelolth's plan, I realized. She was responsible for the egg and must have known Connor would bring it to town. She wanted to build an army of shaddim from the people I cared about most. Then I would have nowhere to hide.

—Blow it, Dragonsbane!— Talon repeated. Her words weren't a suggestion. —Wake the town.—

I didn't argue. The sludgemites were spreading too quickly. I had to wake the people of Tiller's Field or they'd all be turned into shaddim.

5

Vwarrrrr—Ooooom!

The Horn's blast shattered glass and uprooted fence posts. Apple trees lost their fruit, and stacks of firewood toppled over. Closest to me, Sheriff Logan's shed collapsed.

If the citizens of Tiller's Field hadn't been awake, they were now. Lanterns and candles suddenly flared in nearby windows. Dogs barked and whined.

Talon squawked to get my attention. —Run! The sludgemites must not catch you.—

I blinked, slowly lowering the Horn and attaching it to my belt. Even with only three of its four pieces, the Horn was awesome. I could still hear its breathtaking howl echoing in my ears.

"*Th*-they're gone," I gasped. Not a single sludgemite remained in sight. Not one clump of slime stuck to the grass. "We're safe."

Talon swooped in to hover inches from my face. Her

slitted eyes stared into mine. —You will never be safe as long as you carry the Horn. It was broken for a reason.—

I blinked again. I'd never thought of that. Why *had* the Horn been broken? Was it more dangerous?

With all four pieces, it had the power to charm and control dragons, but that wasn't much of a threat. Not unless you were a dragon.

"I don't…" I muttered, shaking my head. There was so much I didn't know about the Horn. I'd worked hard to rescue it, but I still didn't know much about it.

If Talon knew more, she wasn't ready to share. —Go into the house. Find your uncle before the sludgemites return.—

Flizzzzdt! The faint sound of sticky wings told me hurry. The 'mites were coming back.

I dashed toward Sheriff Logan's house, heading for the front door. Climbing through the window wasn't necessary this time. I'd already awakened everyone in town. Around the corner, I stopped dead in my tracks.

Ooowhooo-ooh-ooo.

A chilling moan made the hairs on the back of my neck stand up. I knew that sound. I heard it wailing in my dreams. It belonged to a shaddim on the prowl.

I spun wildly in search of the monster. A deserted street stretched to my left and right. There was no sign of the shaddim.

"Where? *Where!*" I gasped, still spinning and squinting. Where was it?

Ooowhooo-ooh-ooo.

The shaddim was close, almost on top of me. I smelled the stench of its breath, the rotten stink of decaying, wet leaves. Where was it?

Skrawt! —Above you!—

I didn't think about Talon's warning. I just acted. My head shot up and my arms followed. The bucket of water went with them.

Overhead a black shadow descended on black wings. Burning eyes blazed from a flame-shaped skull.

The shaddim was a midnight ghost. Wispy trails of dark mist streaked the air when it moved. Starlight shone through its hollow mouth. It had no depth, only width and height like a flat painting.

"Take that!" I shouted, thinking of how the egg's slime had drenched me.

Skloosh! A perfect shot. The bucket and water collided with the shaddim, soaking the monster.

Vrrreeeeeet!

The shaddim squealed and ricocheted in mid-air as if it had crashed into an invisible wall. It spun helplessly out of control, shrinking rapidly as it vanished into the darkness.

There were two things shaddim couldn't stand. Bright light and water. I'd used both to escape them before, but they hadn't had wings then. I doubted that crossing a river

29

or pond would stop them now that they could fly.

Thank goodness for Sheriff Logan's bucket!

That was something else about the shaddim. They were always changing and getting stronger. At first they'd been just ghosts, terrifying enough. Then they had ridden humongous shadow-tooth cats with fangs as long as my arm. Now they had wings.

What was next, fire breathing?

The door to Sheriff Logan's house burst open, and my uncle and the sheriff charged out with weapons and torches in hand.

"Jasiah, what happened?" Uncle Arick demanded. His eyes paused on me long enough to see that I was unharmed, then they flickered warily back and forth.

"Why did you blow the Horn, son?" Sheriff Logan added. He wasn't as big as my uncle but he looked equally danger-ous. His clothes and hair were almost as dark as a shaddim.

"*Th*-the egg," I stammered, barely able to get my words out. My heart was racing and my mouth felt sticky and dry. "The egg hatched. *S*-sludgemites came out. They're *t*-turning everyone into shaddim."

Uncle Arick nodded grimly. "We should have been more careful. Bringing that egg here was exactly what Shelolth wanted."

Sometimes I hated being right. I'd thought that finding

30

the egg had been more than dumb luck. It had. It had been bad luck and a trap.

How many more traps has Shelolth set for us? I couldn't help wondering.

"Take this and stay behind us," my uncle growled, offering me his torch. "We have to move quickly."

That was one reason I liked Uncle Arick so much. He immediately knew what had to be done in every situation. I don't know what I'd do if anything ever happened to him.

I liked the fact that he didn't lecture me right away for checking on the egg, too. I'd made a mistake and we both knew it. We'd talk about it when the danger was over.

The three of us jogged around the house toward the collapsed shed. Sheriff Logan groaned when he saw his destroyed shed, but didn't say anything.

I probably deserved a lecture from him, too.

"The egg must be destroyed before more sludgemites hatch," Uncle Arick said, staring at the ruined shed. "Please help me find it."

For the next several minutes, we dragged boards, weapons, and thatch away from the pile. I thought we'd be better off hunting the sludgemites that had already escaped, but I trusted my uncle. If he said we needed to destroy the egg, then it was my job to ask if he'd like scrambled, over easy, or sunny-side-up.

"*Aha!*" Sheriff Logan suddenly cried. "Here's one." He

raised his boot to squish a sludgemite.

"No!" Uncle Arick exclaimed. "Stop! You touch it, it touches you. The result is the same."

Sheriff Logan froze much as I had earlier, his foot in the air. "Now what?" he asked. Even with a sludgemite inches away, there was no fear in his voice.

Uncle Arick tossed aside the board in his hand and slowly crept across the pile. For such a big man, he could move as silently as a cat. He drew his sword just as quietly and took aim near the sheriff's foot.

"No thank you," Logan joked with a wry smile. "I clipped my toenails yesterday."

My uncle's eyes widened. "*Shhh!*" he hissed too late. Alerted by the combination of noise and movement, the sludgemite jumped. Ooze-coated wings sputtered.

Flizzzzdt!

Uncle Arick yelped and drew back his arm. There on his wrist perched a slimy slug of a sludgemite. One juicy antenna stroked his bare arm.

He turned to me, his face grey and sickly. "Run!" he gasped.

Uncle Arick was still clutching his forearm when he collapsed. Then he lay on his back without moving and stared at the sky with dead eyes. He looked like a corpse awaiting burial.

I backed up, my mouth working but no words coming out. One of the most horrible things I could imagine had just happened. I'd lost my uncle to the sleep of the shaddim. Soon he would wake as a monster.

Uncle Arick was supposed to be invincible. I'd seen him battle shaddim, and heard stories of how he'd single-handedly defeated a sea monster. That some slimy insect had gotten the best of him was unthinkable.

Right then, the Dragonsbane Horn and my quest didn't seem to matter. I'd done everything I could to protect the Horn, but none of it had saved Uncle Arick.

Without realizing what I was doing, I tore the Horn from my belt. I wanted to be rid of it. To throw it so far away that no one would ever find it again.

"I hate you!" I screamed at it, cocking my arm back.

Sheriff Logan caught my wrist. "Go to Wizard Ast," he said firmly. "Talk to him, then decide. This is not over."

I knew that the sheriff was trying to help, but I didn't want to hear it then. Him pulling my arm only made me feel more helpless and angry. Tears welled in my eyes, and I forcibly tore free, turned, and started running down the street.

—I am with you— Talon whispered softly, but I didn't listen to her either. I just ran.

People wearing nightclothes shuffled aimlessly through the streets. Most looked confused, tired, and nervous. Some recognized me and called out.

"Jasiah, what's happening?" Mr. Sootbeard, the black-smith, asked, scratching his balding head.

"Where you going in such a hurry, lad?" inquired Pa Gnobbles, the oldest resident of Tiller's Field.

"We believe in you, Jasiah!" Widow Marmelmaid shouted encouragingly. She was the second oldest resident of the town.

Her words stopped me dead in my tracks. *We believe in you.* Hearing those words stung me deep inside, and I felt ashamed. I was behaving like a quitter and a coward.

The quest for the Dragonsbane Horn wasn't only about my uncle and me. It was about Widow Marmelmaid, Sheriff Logan, and the rest of the people from Tiller's

Field. It was about people everywhere.

Shelolth and her shaddim didn't care about towns, names, or places on a map. They wanted the Horn and would stop at nothing to get it. They would bring their war to anyone or anywhere that stood in their way.

Uncle Arick had already fallen. How many more people would fall if I gave up?

I wiped away my tears and took a deep breath. Tiller's Field needed me. The Horn needed me. I couldn't abandon my quest.

"Light fires!" I cried, waving my arms and starting back down the street. "Shaddim are coming! Light fires!"

Light was our only hope. The shaddim couldn't be stopped by weapons or strength.

Townsfolk crowded around me, asking questions and looking for reassurance. *Would they be safe indoors? When would I blow the Horn to chase away the monsters?* Few of them really understood what was happening. Even fewer were prepared to fight.

"Please, let me through," I pleaded. "I have to warn the rest of the town."

I tried to politely squeeze past the crowd but anxious faces greeted me at every turn. Nothing worked until—
Ooowhooo-ooh-ooo.

A teeming pack of shaddim materialized from the night. They swept forward on shapeless wings with their skinny arms outstretched like zombies. Swarms of sludgemites

35

followed them like moths to flame.

I quit struggling. Not every torch, candle, and lantern in Tiller's Field would be enough to drive a pack that size away.

7

Ooowhooo-ooh-ooo.

The shaddim moaned and the crowd fell back, terrified and stunned. My warnings hadn't prepared them for this. Not for bloodthirsty monsters invading their home.

"Do as Jasiah says!" Mr. Sootbeard bellowed. "Get torches and lanterns—anything that burns!" Next to him, his big dog, Thorn, barked and growled.

Some of the townsfolk turned and fled. Some ran back to their homes. Very few lit fires and stood their ground.

—You must escape— Talon hissed sharply. —This is not a battle you can win. The town is lost.—

I glanced up to see the wyvern high overhead, a speck against the night sky. "No!" I cried with more feeling than I expected. "I am not a coward!"

Talon dove in low enough for me to see her shining eyes. —Cowards refuse to fight, but only fools look for war.—

I met her gaze defiantly. "Then I'm a fool!" I snapped. "Now are you my Companion or not?"

The colorful feathers along Talon's neck ruffled in irritation. —Of course, Dragonsbane. I will fight *and* die with you.—

Her words stung as much a Widow Marmelmaid's had. First I'd been trying to run away from responsibility. Now I was running blindly into it. Allowing the shaddim to catch me and steal the Horn wouldn't help anyone.

"Look!" Mr. Sootbeard exclaimed before I could respond to Talon. "There's the sheriff."

A hopeful cheer rose from what was left of the crowd. The people believed that if anyone could defeat the shaddim, it was Sheriff Logan. Lucky for them they hadn't seen what had happened to my uncle.

The sheriff charged toward the oncoming shaddim, his cloak flapping like a banner. Close behind him sprinted four others—Deputy Josh, Enchantress Jozlyn, Page Connor, and Apprentice Simon. The four were the young heroes of Tiller's Field and some of my best friends.

"Now, Simon!" Jozlyn shouted. "Start the spell!"

Simon responded by skidding to a halt and pushing up his sleeves. With his arms wide, he chanted.

Obey me, air, as I command.
Convey thee, snare, 'cross sky and land.

When Simon lowered his arms, a warm breeze started to swirl around my ankles, making me feel as if I'd stepped into a draining bathtub. The air rose quickly and then lashed out as fast as a dragon's tail.

Wind howled down the street, throwing up dust and knocking over potted plants. Shutters flapped and flags snapped. Simon's robe started to flutter.

"Your turn!" Simon called to Jozlyn. The sound of his voice was almost lost in the rush of the wind and the moaning of the approaching shaddim.

Jozlyn nodded and held back her long hair with one hand. The wind was whipping everywhere now. Even the shaddim had slowed with it blowing in their faces.

Clutching a miniature broom at her waist, Jozlyn added a spell of her own to Simon's magic.

Betray shape, breeze, become a box.
Delay 'scape, please, with walls and locks.

Jozlyn ended her chant by sweeping her broom over her head and drawing a box shape with it in the air. When she completed the square, heavy silence filled the street as if the whole area had been locked inside an air tight tomb.

The wind stopped blowing and the shaddim stopped moaning. What had Simon and Jozlyn done?

"Quick—more fire!" Sheriff Logan cried. Somehow he was in the middle of the crowd. I hadn't seen him leave the others. "Form a ring and stay inside. The spells won't hold long."

He glanced over his shoulder and down the street. Jozlyn and Simon were running full steam toward us. Josh and Connor walked slowly backward in the same direction, swords in hand. Josh's blade burned with blue fire.

Amazingly, the shaddim didn't follow. Their mouths opened to moan but no sound came out. Their wings flapped but seemed unable to carry them past some invisible line. It was as if they were trapped in a soundproof cage.

That was it! Simon and Jozlyn had used magic to create a box of solid air around the shaddim. That's why I couldn't hear them and why they didn't give chase. The monsters were trapped.

I hugged Jozlyn and Simon when they arrived. The two of them just might have saved Tiller's Field. "Nice work!" I beamed.

"Our pleasure," they huffed breathlessly together.

Josh and Connor came next. I hugged Josh but Connor only offered me his hand. When I took it, he hauled me in for a surprise bear hug. "I'm glad you're all right, peasant."

I gave him a friendly shove. That was just like Connor. Always calling people peasant.

Vwarrr-ooowhooo-ooh-ooo.

A terrifying noise interrupted our reunion. It sounded like a mix between the Dragonsbane Horn and a shaddim's moan.

41

The crowd spun as one and gasped in horror. A second, larger pack of shaddim had sneaked up behind us. In their lead floated a barrel-chested figure with bulging arms and a lower half that trailed into mist. A wild mane of smoke hung to its shoulders like hair.

That was no regular shaddim. That was—

"Uncle Arick?" I gasped, stumbling forward.

The impressive figure floated closer. It gripped a smoky war horn the same size as the Dragonsbane Horn in one fist. Around that fist was a gauntlet just like mine.

"Your uncle is gone, whelp," the figure hissed menacingly. *"I am Arick Shadowmane. Give the Horn to me."*

When a dark shadow blotted out the sky, I knew it was the end.

8

Grr-RARRRG!

The massive shadow plummeted from above, roaring deafeningly. The force of the noise shook buildings and flattened most of the crowd. Even Arick Shadowmane and the nearby shaddim were sent gliding helplessly backward.

"CLEAR A PATH OR SUFFER MY WEIGHT!" the shadow bellowed. "I INTEND TO LAND."

My head shot up in surprise as the townsfolk scattered. The shadow could roar and speak?

I got my first good look at it then and realized something terribly important. The shadow wasn't a shadow. It was a dragon.

Crimson scales and bone-white horns flashed past. Yellow fangs longer than the Dragonsbane Horn parted to let loose a second roar.

Grr-RARRRG!

Flakes of ash filled the air, and the peppery scent of burnt wood clogged my nostrils. The dragon hadn't breathed its awful fire yet, but I was already gasping for air.

—Agamemnon— Talon whispered in awe. —Isn't he handsome?—

Agamemnon? I wondered. *Talon knows the dragon's name?*

I forced my eyes away from the huge dragon and spotted Talon. She hovered near a rooftop, staring intensely at the dragon. Her scales flushed with pink as if she were blushing.

"*Handsome?*" I sneered. "You've got to be kidding. That thing's a monster."

Talon didn't look away from the dragon. —No more monster than I. Agamemnon is a noble among dragondom.—

Whoops! I had really put my foot in my mouth that time. Calling Agamemnon a monster was almost the same as calling Talon a monster. Dragons and wyverns were closely related.

"Sorry, Talon," I said lamely. "I didn't mean …"

"Dragonsbane," Agamemnon rumbled as he landed with a booming thump. His voice had quieted, sounding like a boulder tumbling downhill instead of a full-blown earth-quake. "It is time to go."

I scrambled to my feet and scooted backward, nearly tripping over my friends. "*G*-go where?"

Agamemnon couldn't be trusted. No dragon could, not

around me especially. I was the Dragonsbane, the rival of dragons everywhere. A dragon helping me would be like a mouse setting its own mousetrap.

"Bah!" the dragon growled. "You humans are as timid as deer. I expected more from the so-called Dragonsbane."

That did it. I was tired of being pushed around. The shaddim had taken my uncle and now a dragon was insulting me. I'd had enough.

I snatched the Horn from my belt and shook it in front of Agamemnon's long snout. The shaking part was easy. I was so terrified that I couldn't have held steady if I'd wanted to. "I am the Dragonsbane and the Horn obeys me. So will you if I blow it."

In the time it takes to sneeze, Agamemnon whipped out a clawed hand and caught me firmly. My arms and the Horn were pinned to my sides. I couldn't move. So much for being the Dragonsbane.

Agamemnon sucked in a deep breath as if summoning his fire. He reared back his head and—

"Wait!"

A girl's voice froze the dragon and me. Then the girl appeared, scrambling over the ridges on Agamemnon's back. Next to her bounded an oversized mutt of a dog.

"*E*-Emily?" I croaked in disbelief, unable to get a good breath in Agamemnon's grasp. Now I was really confused. What were my friend Emily and her dog Leland doing on the dragon's back?

Emily waved excitedly. She was a tall girl who always wore her red hair in a ponytail. She carried a bow over one shoulder and usually dressed in what some people would call "boy's clothes." *Tomboy* was a good word to describe her.

"Quit playing and get up here," she said. "We have a long way to fly today."

I sputtered, still struggling to breathe. *Quit playing?* Ten seconds earlier Agamemnon had been getting ready to roast me alive!

The dragon chuckled thunderously and steam puffed from his nostrils. "The boy has much to learn," he stated plainly. Then he hoisted me onto his back, plunking me down next to Emily.

"Hi, Jasiah," a surprise voice said from behind me. I turned to find Emily's best friend, Daniel, reclining on the dragon's back with his feet up. "You were almost a human barbeque," he joked.

Daniel was always calling stuff a human *something* or other. Climb a tree and you were a human squirrel. Jump a hole and you were a human leapfrog. Sometimes I thought Daniel was a human motor mouth.

He, Emily, and Leland were from a nearby town called Willowhill. They were heroes there like Jozlyn and my friends were heroes here. They had come to join me on the quest for the fourth and final piece of the Dragonsbane Horn.

"Jasiah, are you safe?" Sheriff Logan called. He was the first one brave enough to approach the dragon.

"Yes," I shouted back. "Are you?" I'd suddenly remembered the shaddim, sludgemites, and my uncle. There was still trouble even though the dragon wasn't going to eat me.

"It's dawn, lad," the sheriff smiled. "The shaddim are gone. Once you depart ..."

He didn't have to finish the sentence. I knew what he meant. Once I left, Tiller's Field would be safe again. The shaddim would be busy hunting me.

"Goodbye," I said simply. It was time for me to go and there was no sense in drawing it out.

My friends on the ground and the other townsfolk waved as Agamemnon crouched then sprang into the air. We were on our way.

Free to Choose

Agamemnon soared up at a steep angle, and my stomach
dropped straight down. I felt like the rope in a game of
tug-of-war between the sky and the earth. I wanted to
scream but couldn't open my mouth.

Daniel noticed the sour look on my face. "First time on a
dragon?" he smirked.

First and last time, I thought. But to Daniel all I could
do was jerk my head in a quick nod.

Emily shot him a disapproving look then smiled at me.
"It'll get easier once we level off. Just keep your eyes
closed for now." Leland barked cheerfully in agreement,
his bushy brown and yellow tail wagging.

Nice! I thought. *The dog is having the time of his life,
but I'm supposed to put my tail between my legs and hide.*

Leland was a big dog, but I couldn't tell what kind. His
head reached my chest when we were standing. Maybe he
was part giant.

"I'll be … all right," I managed to growl through

clenched teeth. I wanted to smile at Emily but was afraid the wind would catch in my cheeks and set my lips to flapping.

I hung on and kept my eyes focused on the dragon's back until he leveled off. No way was I going to shut them for more than a blink. Not with everyone watching.

To my relief, Agamemnon finally dipped his head and gave one last powerful thrust of his wings. My stomach fell again, and then we were gliding smoothly forward, level with the ground.

My outlook changed instantly, and my heart pounded with pure excitement. I took my first deep breath in what seemed like ages, reared back my head, and howled.

There's nothing quite like flying on a dragon. The ground looks like a colorful checkerboard far below, and the sky stretches on forever. The experience explains the meaning of the expression *on top of the world*.

Emily, Daniel, and Leland shared my excitement. The kids turned their heads from side to side, marveling at the sights. Leland sat near the edge with his big face turned to the wind and his tongue hanging out.

Seeing them made me laugh. After the night I'd had, a little joy went a long way.

"I bet you never thought you'd be a human humming-bird," Daniel smirked, flapping his arms crazily.

The gesture was silly, but I flapped my arms, too, and

laughed some more. I felt completely safe and intensely alive.

This is what it means to be a dragon, I realized, knowing I'd never look at them the same way.

Dragons were ferocious, powerful, and dangerous. They also had no love for people. By most definitions, they were monsters. But they were so much more than that. They were one thing everyone wanted to be.

They were free.

I glanced down at the Horn on my hip. With one blow, I could tame the freest of creatures. I could control any dragon. That was an awesome power. Did I have the right to use it?

—*You have a choice to make*— Agamemnon said suddenly in my mind, the same way Talon spoke to me. The ability to talk like that must be shared by all dragondom.

"What do you mean?" I whispered, feeling an unexpected chill. But I was stalling, trying to hide my thoughts. I knew what Agamemnon meant. He'd been reading my thoughts.

—*The Horn, Dragonsbane. You will have to choose.*—

This time I didn't ask another dumb question. Agamemnon knew what was on my mind, and I knew what he meant about a choice. When the time came, would I use the Horn against him?

Late in the afternoon, a sparkling on the horizon slowly

took shape. We were approaching the Glittersgold Mountains. Roads of pure silver wound around those mountains like shimmering rivers.

"I know this place," I said excitedly. "Silvermight is down there. That's where I found the second piece of the Horn."

Agamemnon raised his bulky head. "We are not stopping. Pirate greed for dragon gold is legendary."

Emily and Daniel stared doubtfully at the mountains. "There are pirates down there?" Emily asked.

"It's a long story," I told her. "But I found this, too." From my backpack, I fished out a silver spyglass covered with images of treasure chests, sailing ships, and the Dragonsbane Horn.

Daniel shrugged, unimpressed. "Looks like an old spyglass. I have one here somewhere ..." He started rummaging through the pockets sewn into the lining of his cloak.

"This one's magic," I said a bit defensively. "I got it from a pirate named Captain Halfhand. It's called Halfhand's Eye."

At hearing the word *magic*, Daniel brought his head up. "Let me see it," he requested.

I passed the spyglass to him and he held it to his eye. "Wow!" he exclaimed immediately. "There are words in here. It knows what things are."

I bit my tongue to keep from saying, *Told you so*. Halfhand's Eye worked like a regular spyglass, but it also named everything it spied. It could even spot buried treasure. That's why a pirate had valued it.

Daniel suddenly laughed. "It calls you a thief!" he hooted, gazing at me thought the spyglass.

"What? Let me see that." I'd never thought to point Halfhand's Eye at myself.

Sure enough, when I peered through the glass with it aimed at my legs, an upsetting message appeared as if written in ink.

Jasiah Dragonsbane

Thief

Wanted Dead or Alive

1,000 Gold Crowns

"One thousand gold," I muttered, lowering the Eye. That was almost enough to buy a whole town the size of Tiller's Field. Plenty to send every fortune hunter after me.

"What's a thousand gold?" Emily wondered.

"It's a reward—a price on my head," I whispered. Another sudden chill caused me to shiver. As if I didn't have enough to worry about already. Now someone wanted me dead or alive.

Skywatch

10

"It'll be all right," Emily said encouragingly. "We've got Leland. No one can sneak up on him." The big dog yipped as Emily scratched his head.

She was trying to be helpful, but I still couldn't keep from worrying. A thousand gold crowns wasn't something to shrug off or ignore. Someone was willing to pay a fortune for my capture, or worse. I couldn't pretend it wasn't true.

"Don't forget Thornwake and Riverwind," Daniel added without his usual smirk. He knew when it was time for jokes and when to be serious.

Thornwake and Riverwind were magical weapons. Daniel and Emily had gotten them on an adventure while battling terrible snow beasts. Thornwake was Daniel's dagger, and Riverwind was Emily's bow.

"You're always looking for a fight," Emily scolded Daniel. "There are other solutions to problems, you know." She wasn't a coward. Far from it. I'd never seen anyone

53

better with a bow. She was just more cautious than Daniel. That made them a good team.

"Whatever, Emi," Daniel replied, rolling his eyes. *Emi* was his nickname for her, and she pretended not to like it. "Sometimes the only thing the bad guys want is a fight."

Before a real argument broke out between them, I stepped in. "All right, all right. I'll quit worrying. You two watch my back, and I'll watch yours."

Leland barked sharply in protest.

"You *three*," I corrected quickly, smiling at the dog. It seemed Leland was used to being left out, and wouldn't stand for it.

Vraaah-thhh!

Agamemnon suddenly spat a crackling stream of fire from his mouth, and we started to rapidly descend. My stomach jumped into my throat, and I sucked in a sharp breath. My ears felt as if they were plugged with water.

"What's the matter?" I gasped, alarmed. I didn't see any enemies. Why else would the dragon breathe his fire?

"Hot air rises," Agamemnon growled in explanation. Have you not noticed the way smoke and heat always float up? That is what keeps me—and *you*—in the air. To land, I have to let out a little steam." To prove what he'd said, he huffed out a second fiery geyser and we descended faster.

Dragonfire wasn't just a weapon! Dragons needed hot air in their lungs so that their big bodies could fly. They were like hot air balloons.

There was one problem. The more I learned about dragons, the less I thought of them as monsters. How would I ever use the Horn against one now?

We landed on a wide plateau on the far side of the Glittersgold Mountains. Not a single plant clung to the rocky ground, and the wind gusted with such strength that I struggled to keep my balance.

An immense stone tower rose impossibly high from the center of the plateau. Coiled around the column was a carved dragon. It spiraled toward the sky with its mouth open as if hungry to feast on the stars above. A horseshoe-shaped doorway in the dragon's tail led inside the tower.

Emily, Leland, Daniel, and I climbed silently from Agamemnon's back. The dragon-tower took our breath away. None of us had ever that imagined something so tall could be built by human hands.

"Welcome to Skywatch," Agamemnon rumbled. Even he seemed impressed by the tower. "This is where we part."

The dragon's words didn't sink in immediately because I was still gawking at the tower he had called Skywatch. When what Agamemnon had said did sink in, I tore my eyes away.

"You're leaving us?" I asked. "We'll freeze up here at night!" It was true. The sun had set, and the air was getting cold. Autumn isn't the best time of year to be stranded on a wide open mountaintop.

Agamemnon smirked or scowled at me. Maybe both, I couldn't quite tell. "You would not enjoy my method for keeping you warm," he stated honestly.

I shuddered as the phrase *well done* came to mind. I knew exactly how the dragon would warm me. Steamed, roasted, and charbroiled.

"Thank you for bringing us here," Emily interjected quickly. "We'll talk with Wizard Ast soon."

I glanced at Emily. Apparently being stranded here was part of our quest. At least Wizard Ast would be meeting us. He would explain everything.

Agamemnon nodded and then took a huge breath. He spread his wings, crouched, and leaped into the sky. I hated to see him go, but I wasn't exactly sure why. For a lot of reasons, I think.

"Let's go inside," Emily suggested.

"Is Wizard Ast in the tower?" I asked.

Daniel chuckled. "Not yet," he said mysteriously. The boy winked at Emily before sprinting off toward the tower.

Not yet, I repeated silently. That meant the wizard was on his way. I shrugged, pretending not to care that Daniel and Emily shared a secret. Wizard Ast would explain that, too.

Taking one last look way up the tower, I followed Daniel toward the doorway in the dragon's tail.

Enter the Dragon

11

I stepped through the doorway in the dragon's tail into a silent, dark world. The sound of the wind howling across the plateau hushed. The light from the stars vanished.

"*D*-Daniel?" I called quietly, urgently. He'd been right ahead of me. Now he was gone.

I closed my eyes and counted to five, giving them time to adjust to the darkness. When I opened them, I saw that I was in a tunnel-shaped room, like a big barrel lying on its side. A curved stone staircase led up into darkness.

The dragon is hollow! I realized in surprise. I'd expected it to be a decoration. I'd thought that the real tower would be straight up and down in the middle. Now I knew the truth. The dragon was the tower, and the stairway led to the top far, far above.

Emily appeared next to me with Leland at her side. "That's a lot of stairs," she observed.

I nodded, not too eager to begin climbing. "Daniel must've started up already," I added.

Emily smiled as if I'd said something funny. "No," she disagreed, peering into the darkness. "He's here somewhere." She spun slowly, then pointed at a clump of shadows near the doorway. "There!"

Smirking, Daniel stepped from the shadows as suddenly as a ghost floating through a brick wall. "Took you long enough," he said.

I gawked at him, amazed. Normally my eyes don't miss a thing, especially a thing as big as a person. But I'd walked right past Daniel without noticing him.

I'd *looked* right at him without noticing!

"How'd you do that?" I gaped.

Daniel held up one side of his cloak, covering his face up to his eyes. "I'm a human chameleon," he whispered in a spooky voice from behind the cloak.

Emily swatted him playfully, knocking the cloak from his grasp. "More like a human *comedian*," she laughed. "Now let's get going."

Sometimes I count stairs while climbing them. Sometimes I sprint up, taking two at a time. But not this climb. I concentrated on putting one foot in front of the other.

The stairway went on forever. Up, up, up. There was no fun in counting or sprinting. After five minutes, I was huffing for breath. After ten, my thighs ached for rest.

"We're human mountain goats," Daniel complained. Still the stairs went on.

"I sure hope … the last piece of the Horn … is at the top," I panted. Riding a dragon had its uncomfortable moments, but they were nothing compared to the discomfort of climbing one.

Finally the tunnel widened and the stairs ended. In fact, the whole tower ended. We'd reached the top of Skywatch.

We were in an oval-shaped room that opened to the sky on the far side. Pointy columns like stalactites and stalagmites formed an odd open wall or window.

"We're in the mouth!" Emily exclaimed, the first to understand.

"Huh?" Daniel and I grunted together.

Emily tapped one of the pointy columns. "These are teeth," she explained. "And that's—" She started toward the far side of the room and the open wall, but turned around quickly, her face pale.

"And that's a long way down," she murmured.

Daniel caught on immediately. "You're not afraid of heights, are you, Emi? We just rode a dragon all day long." He stepped toward the opening but stopped before getting halfway across the room. "Never mind," he whispered, turning back.

We were at the top of Skywatch, in the open mouth of the stone dragon. Through the dragon's parted teeth we could see exactly how high up we really were. It wasn't a pleasant sight.

The mountains plunged straight down, forming a sheer wall that bordered some kind of valley. Dark ash hung in the air below us like thick storm clouds, and eerie red and orange light flashed in the clouds. We couldn't see the ground.

One look was enough for me. Like Emily and Daniel, I turned hurriedly away. "So where's Wizard Ast?" I asked, trying to get my mind on something other than what I'd just seen.

Back at the top of the stairs, as far from the dragon's open mouth as possible, Emily pulled a large blue bottle from her backpack. "He's been with us the whole time," she said.

I stared at the bottle. It didn't have a cap or cork. "What's that?" I'd seen magical creations called efreet that were stored in bottles, but they weren't alive, much less real people.

"Wizard Ast can come to us through the bottle," Daniel said. "He's probably in his tower right now."

I shook my head, still not understanding completely. "Do we break the bottle to let him out?" I asked doubtfully.

Emily and Daniel shared a worried glance. "No," Emily said hurriedly. "You're supposed to say some magic words. He told us that you knew them."

I studied her freckled face for a moment. She was telling the truth.

The problem was, I didn't know any magic words. I wasn't a wizard. How was I going to free Wizard Ast from the bottle?

Magic Words

12

"Say all the magic words you know," Daniel suggested. He was trying to be helpful but was wasting his breath. I didn't know the first thing about magic.

I shrugged helplessly and sat down with a sigh. Why did Wizard Ast expect me to know magic? I was just a regular kid. There wasn't really anything special about me except my last name.

"I don't know any magic words," I admitted.

Emily frowned in thought and Daniel squinted. "But Wizard Ast told us that only you could make the bottle work," Daniel said. "You have to know the words. *Think.*"

Daniel still wasn't helping. He was just putting me under more pressure.

"*Shhh!*" I hissed a bit rudely. "Let me think."

I'd been around people who used magic. Mostly my friends Jozlyn and Simon, and of course Wizard Ast. Maybe if I concentrated, I would remember one of their spells.

—Give up yet?—

Thinking so hard, I flinched a the sound of Talon's voice. I hadn't heard from her since we'd left Tiller's Field that morning.

"Where have you been?" I asked silently.

—Guarding you, of course— the wyvern replied.

I rolled my eyes, hoping Emily and Daniel wouldn't notice. They'd think I was talking to myself.

"That's your answer—guarding me?" I thought to Talon. *"That doesn't tell me much."*

—Dragons are not fond of wyverns. It was best for me to remain unseen.—

That sounded serious, so I decided not to pry. *"All right then, what do you know about magic words?"* I asked instead.

Talon hissed a chuckle. —As much as you do, I'm sure.—

Well, that's not very much then, I grumbled, not meaning to share the thought with Talon.

To my surprise, she heard anyway. I'd forgotten that she could read my mind anytime she wanted.   —You're wrong. You have the magic words memorized.—

I was about to snap at her when I suddenly remembered something. I did know a magic poem. I knew the legend of the Dragonsbane Horn.

"Let me see the bottle," I requested of Emily. When she

passed it over, I quietly repeated the legend.

> One waits with the wizard
> In his hollow tome.
> One sounds in the sands
> Of the dwarven home.
> One rings wrapped in roots
> In damp forest loam.
> One drones in the dark
> Where the shaddim roam.

> Four for the future.
> Four 'fore the reign.
> Four for the forging
> Of Horn Dragonsbane.

I finished and stared hopefully at the bottle. I expected smoke to start pouring out. I expected the wizard to appear like a genie. I expected something to happen. But nothing did.

"Come on!" I exclaimed, shaking the bottle in both hands. "Please! I don't know any more magic words."

Glurk!

The bottle suddenly hiccupped and a wisp of blue smoke puffed into the air. I held my breath, but the smoke drifted apart uneventfully. Wizard Ast did not appear.

"Quick!" Daniel urged. "Repeat what you just said."

"The whole poem?" I asked.

"No, what you said after."

I shrugged bewilderedly. "*Um ...* I don't know any more magic words." I was guessing. I couldn't remember exactly what I'd said.

Emily shook her head, and her ponytail flopped back and forth. "You started with 'Come on,' then said—"

"Please!" I cried excitedly. The bottle hiccupped again. "Please, please!" I repeated.

Every time I said the word *please*, the bottle hiccupped and let out more smoke. But that's as far as it got, little plumes of smoke appearing and drifting apart. I was more frustrated than ever.

"I give up," I sighed. "I'm sorry I ever laid eyes on this bottle." I was about to send it rolling down the stairway when it hiccupped again.

Glurk!

"There!" Daniel cried. "You said more magic words. *I'm sorry.*" Leland barked, agreeing with him.

My jaw almost fell open. Could the riddle be that simple? The bottle wasn't waiting for a wizard's magic words but for *the* magic words. The words everyone learns by the time they're five years old. *Please, I'm sorry, and—*

"Thank you!" I shouted. Leland woofed again, obviously pleased.

Glurk! Glurk! Glurk!

The bottle hiccupped several times in a row. It sounded as if liquid was being poured too quickly. Then the bottle

66

started to vibrate so rapidly that it squirted from my grasp like a wet bar of soap.

I cried out, clawing after it, but the bottle didn't fall. It floated up above our heads and rotated, sending out a steady stream of blue smoke. We soon lost sight of the bottle.

"Is this how it's supposed to work?" I asked.

"I don't ... *cough* ... know," Emily wheezed. The smoke was getting thick.

Bloip!

A sudden smacking sound like a loud, wet kiss popped somewhere in the smoke, and then the bottle slowly reappeared. Two swollen-looking, red lips that hadn't been there before sprouted from the bottle's opening.

The lips parted. "Are you sure-certain that you spoke all-every one of the magic words?" asked a voice that sound exactly like Wizard Ast's.

13

"What have I done?" I cried in horror. Wizard Ast was trapped in the magic bottle. Only his lips stuck through the narrow opening at the top.

"Pardon-excuse me?" the lips asked in the wizard's usual doublespeak. "I cannot hear well with you out there and my ears stuck-confined in here."

Daniel leaped to his feet and shouted at the bottle. "What can we do to help you?"

Even though Daniel was red in the face, Wizard Ast hadn't seemed to hear him. "I wonder how you can help-aid me," he thought aloud.

"That's what I said!" Daniel shouted.

"Hmm-what?" Wizard Ast's lips asked.

"That's what—forget it," Daniel huffed.

"Let me try-attempt something," the wizard's lips mumbled.

Vlurp! Suddenly the lips popped back into the bottle. Then *bloot!* an ear appeared where the lips had been.

"Can you hear us now?" Emily asked hopefully.

"*My man mear moo!*" Wizard Ast mumbled, sounding very far away. We could barely hear him, and his words didn't make any sense.

"*Fan foo fear fee?*" he continued.

I threw up my arms helplessly. "We can't understand you," I groaned. Emily and Daniel shrugged in agreement.

"*Gibbet-gloat!*" Wizard Ast sighed.

Squirp! The ear vanished with a slippery sound, then the whole bottle started to shake. A sound like pounding hammers mixed with cutting saws boomed from the opening. The noise reminded me of kids building a tree fort.

"What's happen—?" Daniel started, but a new noise cut him off.

Vwip! A pointed wizard's hat and a clump of white hair squirted from the bottle. *Sprott!* Then a wrinkled forehead, two bushy eyebrows, and two eyes appeared.

"You can do it!" I shouted, and one of the bright eyes winked. Then both closed in concentration and—

BROOP! Wizard Ast's whole head popped out. It sprouted from the top of the bottle like a blooming flower from a vase.

"Huzzah-hooray!" the wizard cheered. "Free at last."

Emily, Daniel, and I didn't say a word. Leland whimpered and flattened his ears against his head. Wizard Ast wasn't quite as free as he thought.

He noticed our faces and rolled his eyes crazily like he was trying to spot his own chin. "I'm a wee bit shorter-smaller than I remember," he said seriously.

"You're a human jack-o-lantern," Daniel muttered. "Ow!" he added when Emily socked his arm.

"Now let's not get *a head* of ourselves," Wizard Ast replied just as seriously as before. "*No body* agrees-concurs with you."

A head? No body? Wizard Ast was making jokes at his predicament! Half trapped in the bottle, he was all head and no body.

"Just where is this conversation *headed*?" I laughed.

"I'd sure like a *head's* up," Emily agreed, catching on.

Daniel groaned. "Now who's the comedian? Good thing I got a *head* start."

We could have gone on for hours. But Wizard Ast cleared his throat noisily to let us know that it was time to be serious.

"I'm glad-pleased to see you again," he began after we'd worked out our giggles. "But I do not have long-much time."

I instantly forgot about acting silly. We were on a quest, after all. "Can you tell us where to find the last piece of the Horn?"

Wizard Ast squinted at me. "You already know, Jasiah. Remember-recall the last clue-hint of the legend."

The poem I'd mistaken for magic words came to mind. It was made up of four clues. Since we already had three pieces of the Horn, I went straight to the fourth clue.

One drones in the dark
Where the shaddim roam.

I recited.

"Right-correct," Wizard Ast nodded. The whole bottle tipped back and forth with his nodding head. "The fourth piece is in Hollowdeep, land-home of the shaddim."

A sinking feeling tugged at my stomach. "Hollowdeep is the valley outside, isn't it? That place covered with ash."

Wizard Ast frowned. "I'm afraid so, but do not despair-fear. I have advice-wisdom told to me by your uncle." He cleared his throat again, then recited a short rhyme.

Seek your claim from living flame
Where ashes choke the sky.

Speak the name of dragon fame
The lava can't deny.

"Unfortunately, only your uncle knows-understands the meaning of the words," Ast explained when he'd finished the poem. "It is a Dragonsbane secret-riddle."

The feeling in my stomach tugged harder. Not only had I lost Uncle Arick to shaddim, I'd lost my chance to understand his poem. Its words made no sense to me. *Living flame? Lava?* They sounded dangerous.

"I must go-leave now," Wizard Ast sighed. "The magic of the bottle is fading-weakening."

As he said it, his pointed hat and hair started to drift apart, turning to smoke. "Goodbye-farewell," he called, sounding far away again. "Remember your uncle's words."

Then the wizard's entire head became smoke and disappeared. The magic bottle fell to the floor and clanked loudly, but did not break.

14

Emily snatched Wizard Ast's bottle when it came to a stop and stuffed it into her backpack. "That's that, I guess," she said with a shrug.

"What do you mean?" Daniel asked.

"That I'm not climbing back down those stairs tonight," Emily responded. "Or did you plan on jumping?" She raised one eyebrow.

I heard them talk, but felt strangely far away. I had too much on my mind to really pay attention. The words of Uncle Arick's poem kept repeating in my mind. What did they mean?

About all I could guess was that they were instructions. They described something important that I had to do. Or some *things* that I had to do.

The only question was what? Nothing about the poem made much sense. How could I claim anything from fire?

I finally gave up with a sigh. Maybe the poem would make sense after we reached Hollowdeep. I'd find out tomorrow.

"I'm going to sleep," I announced. There was nothing else to do besides worry and wonder, and those are even less fun than usual while inside a stone dragon's mouth hundreds of feet in the air.

We unrolled blankets from our packs and made camp at the top of the stairs. None of us wanted to be close to the dragon's open mouth. None of us thought to keep watch either.

But we should have.

I took a long time to fall asleep. The worrying and wondering wouldn't let me relax. So when I heard a suspicious sound, I came instantly awake.

Grrrnnnt …

The sound was quiet but close. It reminded me of an old tree swaying in the wind.

I peeked open my eyes but had my back to the dragon's mouth. The noise had come from behind me. All I could see was Leland sleeping on his side.

Maybe I imagined the noise, I tried to convince myself. *Leland should have awakened, too.* My ears were good, but were they better than the dog's?

I closed my eyes for no more than a second when a new sound drifted up from the stairway.

Skritch.

My eyes popped open again. This time I was sure I'd

75

heard something. It was a scratchy crunch, like a booted foot stepping lightly on stone.

Someone was on the stairs!

Leland scrambled to his feet as I threw off my blanket and leaped up. At least he'd heard the sound this time.

"Wake up!" I shouted to Emily and Daniel. Leland barked helpfully, and my friends sat up, looking sleepy and confused.

"*W*-what's happening?" Emily gasped.

"Someone's—!" I started but it was too late.

Thwoonk! In the opening on the other side of the room, a wooden gangplank slammed onto the bottom row of dragon's teeth. Snarling men charged over the plank like bullies struggling to be first in line. They carried weapons in their hands.

"Let's get 'em, mates," a man rasped.

"Find the cap'n's Eye," another growled.

I recognized the gruff voices immediately. The men were pirates. I'd met them while searching for the second piece of the Dragonsbane Horn.

Fingers suddenly snatched my collar, and I screamed. They yanked me around. "The stairs—run!" Emily cried, pushing me.

I started to flee and ran smack into another man. I'd forgotten that the stairway wasn't safe!

"Greetings, m'boy," the pirate hissed. "'Tis me pleasure

76

to be seein' ye again." As he spoke, he poked me in the chest with a hand missing two fingers.

I knew that hand! It belonged to Captain Halfhand, the pirate who wanted me dead or alive.

Check, Mate

15

"Yuck!" Emily gagged when she got her first good look at the pirates. "What are they?"

She'd finally noticed what I knew too well. Captain Halfhand and his crew weren't normal pirates. They weren't even normal men.

They were ghouls.

Their bodies were a disgusting mix of bones, grey flesh, and forgotten treasure. Dusty gems glinted where their eyes should be. Chains, cracked scepters, and crowbars hung from their shoulders instead of arms. Silver peg legs and bars of gold served as their legs and feet.

With surprising speed, the pirates swarmed Emily and me. We kicked and punched, but our blows bounced harmlessly off their bone and metal bodies. We didn't stand a chance against such monsters.

Leland fought, too, snapping at anything that came near. He struggled so valiantly that it took a trio of ghastly crewmen to fit a jeweled muzzle over his jaws. But not before his teeth left their mark.

The pirates tied Emily's and my hands behind our backs. A stiff leash was looped around Leland's neck.

"Now, now, m'boy," Captain Halfhand sneered, "ain't ye glad to see yer old skipper?"

When I didn't answer, Halfhand went on. "Ye gots yerself some new friends, I see. But what happened to that scurvy bird o' yers?" He finished with a smirk, chuckling at some private joke.

He was talking about Talon.

"She's gone," I lied. "She got tired of following me around." But in my mind I called out to her. *"Talon?"* There was no answer.

Captain Halfhand leaned over and thrust his unshaven face close to mine. His breath stank of boiled cabbage, and dull gold teeth filled his mouth. "Is that so?" he growled.

"*S*-she's gone," I repeated unconvincingly.

The gruesome captain scowled, staring deep into my eyes. His lips twitched cruelly in a smile. "I'm afraid we'll have to add lyin' to yer list o' crimes."

He stood up and awkwardly snapped the fingers of his half hand. His other hand and arm was a sharpened stick.

A rotting crewman shuffled up and dropped an oily sack at my feet. It landed with an unpleasant thud. "Care to take a gander inside, boy?" Captain Halfhand taunted.

"A gander!" barked one of his crewmen. "More like a

scurvy bird."

I turned my head away, horrified. I knew what was inside the sack—Talon, unconscious or worse. The pirates had gotten to her before coming after us.

"What do you want with us?" Emily demanded, struggling in the unnatural hands of her captors. "We haven't committed any crimes."

Halfhand tromped over to stand in front of her. "Yer crime is the company ye keep, missy," he snarled. "As for yer friend, he's a thief and a liar."

"But …" Emily started to protest, then looked helplessly at me. I knew she'd suddenly remembered the magical spyglass in my backpack and the price on my head.

I smiled sadly at her. I really was a thief, just like the pirates claimed. Now it was time for me to pay.

"Take 'em to the brig," Captain Halfhand ordered with a wave of his pointy arm. "They'll be walkin' the plank when we get good an' far over Hollowdeep."

The ghoulish crewmen snapped to attention, chains and bones rattling. "Aye, aye, cap'n," they said together. Then they started dragging us toward the gangplank leaning against the dragon's teeth.

"What about their gear?" a crewman asked, prodding our blankets with his peg leg.

The captain cackled. "Aw, ain't that sweet? Three blankets, even one for the dog."

I shot Emily a quick look, and she nodded slightly. The pirates didn't know about Daniel. They thought his blanket belonged to Leland.

But that didn't answer one important question. Where had Daniel gone?

16

The pirate ship hovered next to Skywatch like a bloated dragon. Six misty creatures, called efreet, were chained to the ship's railing. They kept it floating in the air.

The efreet were muscular but ghost-like. They had no waists, legs, or minds, and were really semi-solid spells conjured for pulling ships.

I'd never seen them lift a ship into the sky before. That must be why the pirates needed six of them. Usually one or two was all it took to pull a ship.

Captain Halfhand and his crew, I realized, had invented a dangerous new use for the efreet. They could travel the air just as easily as the seas. Nowhere was out of reach.

The ship itself resembled the pirates. Torn sails fluttered from its masts. Holes gaped in its hull. The name *Restless* was scrawled on its side as if painted in blood.

"She's a beaut', eh, boy?" Halfhand remarked when he noticed me staring at the ship. He jabbed my back with his half hand, shoving me across the gangplank. "Welcome aboard."

Crewmen led Emily, Leland, and I below deck to a cell in a crowded storage room. Chests and boxes brimming with jewels and coins filled the hold from floor to ceiling. Sacks spilled gems onto the floor.

Of course we weren't allowed to investigate. The crewmen silently untied our hands, then locked us in the barred cell. Talon's sack was tossed in with us. Our packs and gear, including Emily's bow, were left to rot among the treasure.

As soon as the pirates climbed the stairs to the surface, Emily removed Leland's muzzle and I untied the sack that held Talon.

"What's in there?" Emily asked.

I drew back the folds of the sack, freeing Talon. Even in the near-dark, she was breathtaking. Her scales gleamed with a beauty that couldn't be found in any of the glittering treasure elsewhere in the room.

"She's beautiful," Emily gasped. "What is she?"

Talon's small chest rose and fell with slow breathing. "She's alive," I smiled, tears coming to my eyes.

"I can see that," Emily grumbled a bit impatiently.

I smiled, wiping my eyes. "Sorry. Talon is my guardian. She's a wyvern. I wear the gauntlet for her." I raised my arm so Emily could see the scratches on my gauntlet.

"She bites you?" Emily frowned.

I couldn't keep from laughing. "No!" I snorted, forgetting where we were for just a minute. "Talon lands on my arm like a trained falcon."

Emily winked. "I know. I was teasing. Think we should try to wake her?"

That sounded like a good idea at first, but I realized that Talon was probably asleep for a reason. Since none of us was going anywhere soon, I decided Talon should rest. I pulled the sack up to her long neck like a blanket, then tiptoed to the other side of the cell.

"What about … the human chameleon?" I whispered to Emily. I meant Daniel but didn't want to say his name out loud. Halfhand and his crew might overhear and discover that one of us was still free.

"Oh, he's around," Emily grinned. "Don't tell me you missed him again?"

"Around where?" I asked, surprised. Hiding in the shadows of Skywatch was one thing. Sneaking around a ship full of undead pirates was another.

Emily didn't answer directly, probably for the same reason I didn't say Daniel's name aloud. "Do you see my bow?" she asked.

I glanced to where the pirates had stashed our gear. Everything was gone, including Riverwind, Emily's bow.

I smiled without speaking, and Emily winked again. Daniel was on the ship and had already rescued our gear. It couldn't be long before he came for us!

So we waited. And waited. The ship creaked and groaned as it sailed throughout the day and into night again.

To pass the time, we played rock-paper-scissors, but that got boring fast. Leland's paws couldn't make any gesture but paper—or maybe rock. We never figured it out.

"I wish you could talk again," Emily sighed at the big dog.

"What?" I gawked. Leland used to talk?

Emily shrugged. "It was on our adventure with the snow beasts. Leland learned to talk. He used it to save my life." She pulled the dog in for a tight hug.

"He knows when to be quiet," Daniel said suddenly.

Emily and I blinked in amazement. Neither of us had seen the dark-haired boy sneaking this time.

Daniel knelt in front of the door to our cell. "Your talking almost got me caught twice today," he muttered.

"We're so glad to—!" I started when a sharp noise interrupted.

Clengk!

The door to our cell swung open.

"I'm a human lock pick," Daniel beamed, tucking some small tools into his cloak. "Now hurry but be quiet. There's a guard on deck."

17

We crept from the cell and onto the stairs as quietly as cats. All of us except Leland, that is. He couldn't creep like a cat no matter how hard he tried.

Daniel led the way. At the top of the stairs, he paused and touched a finger to his lips. Then he pointed to the open hatch above.

Thoont, s-s-scrint.

The sound of a heavy footfall followed by a scuffling noise vibrated the deck overhead. Someone was coming! A pirate walking with a limp.

I turned to scamper back down the stairs, but Daniel grabbed my tunic. "*Wait,*" he mouthed silently.

Thoont, s-s-scrint. The footsteps vibrated louder, closer.

Daniel held up five fingers, and counted them down to the pirate's every step. *Thoont, s-s-scrint.* Four fingers. *Thoont, s-s-scrint.* Three fingers. *Thoont, s-s-scrint.*

When his hand made a fist, he nodded. "Now," he whispered, and took off through the hatch.

Not until then did I realize that the sound of the footsteps had vanished. Daniel had really done his homework. He'd known exactly how many steps it would take the guard to pass.

Emily gently pushed my shoulders to get me moving. "Go," she said directly into my ear. "We don't have much time."

I shot through the hatch and ran immediately into Daniel. Wearing his black cloak, he was almost as dark as a shaddim.

"Careful," he warned. "We're heading for those boxes." He pointed at a cluster of crates stacked messily along the starboard—*right*—railing. An efreet floated nearby, but the creature paid no attention to us.

I nodded and Daniel gave my shoulders a shove the way Emily had. *Is the dog going to push me next?* I wondered as I sprinted for the crates.

In the middle of the stack was a small cubby just big enough for the four of us. We climbed inside, squatted low, and waited for the guard to pass again. I don't know about Emily and Daniel, but I held my breath.

Thoont, s-s-scrint, went the guard's plodding steps.

This time the pirate passed closer than before, and I could make out soft words that he sang in time to his awkward march.

87

For love of gold
I left me home
To sail the Sandy Sea.

The sands took hold,
But still I roam.
A mate is all I be.

The song faded as the pirate lumbered by, and I exhaled slowly. Daniel and Emily did the same.

"There's a dinghy over the rail," Daniel whispered. "Our stuff is already there."

Suddenly Daniel's plan seemed incomplete to me. He wanted us to climb into dinghy that was hundreds of feet in the air. Had he forgotten that we weren't sailing over water?

Emily caught on, too. "You're not thinking of jumping again, are you?" she asked Daniel.

Daniel rolled his eyes as he opened his cloak. He tapped a bottle that dangled from his neck by a leather cord.

"Efreet," he explained. "It should be able to carry the dinghy."

Should be able. Those were dangerous words. If the efreet wasn't strong enough, we'd have a long time falling to regret it.

Emily scrambled over the railing first. Leland bounded after her. "We're safe," she called up a few seconds later.

I had my doubts. A glance over the railing made me think of a lot of things, but safety wasn't one of them.

A blanket of ash swirled sluggishly in the air just below the hull of the ship. It stretched to the horizon in every direction like angry, dark clouds on a stormy night.

Through tiny pockets in the ash, I caught glimpses of the valley of Hollowdeep far below. Streams of glowing lava snaked across the rocky landscape. Not a single tree or plant was anywhere in sight.

"*Ugh,*" I groaned. I couldn't believe we had to go to such a dreary place. Hollowdeep was a wasteland. It reminded me of the nightmare I'd had about destroying the Horn.

"Get ready for adventure," Daniel grinned as he vaulted over the railing.

My turn came next. Sitting in the rear of the dinghy, Daniel was already uncorking the bottle that contained the magical efreet.

"Hurry, Jasiah," Emily urged. "The guard will be back soon." Leland whined in support.

I closed my eyes, took a deep breath, and started for the railing. Now that I had seen what Hollowdeep was, I couldn't help wondering if taking our chances with the pirates wasn't a better idea.

Maybe that thought slowed me. Maybe things happen for a reason. All I know is that when I grasped the railing, a hand missing two fingers clamped tightly onto my shoulder.

"Leavin' without a goodbye, m'boy?" Captain Halfhand sneered.

Awakening Restless

18

The sack that held Talon slipped from my grasp as Captain Halfhand spun me around. Why I hadn't tied it to my belt along with the Horn, I didn't know.

"Got her!" Emily cried from the dinghy, and I sighed with relief. Talon was safe. For the moment.

I wasn't so lucky.

Captain Halfhand and two of his rotting crewmen surrounded me, forcing my back against the railing. The crewmen gripped sabers in their good hands.

"Who's yer new friend?" Halfhand snarled. He meant Daniel. The pirates hadn't seen him before.

"He's the human phantom," I shot back, immediately regretting it. *The human phantom?* Couldn't I come up with something better than that?

Halfhand frowned, probably thinking the same thing I was. He shook his head then turned to his crewmen. "Cut the ropes," he ordered.

"No!" I shrieked, twisting around to the railing. My

friends were trapped in the dinghy. They'd fall if the pirates cut its ropes.

Daniel didn't seem to hear my warning. "Haha!" he cheered, finally uncorking his efreet bottle. Purple mist started to seep and swirl from its opening.

"The ropes!" I yelled, knowing it was too late. "They're cutting the ropes!"

Daniel raised the bottle as Halfhand's crewmen shoved me aside. He spotted them and hurriedly read the words on the bottle's label.

Efreet, you cheat!
Don't hide inside.
Escape, take shape.
Come glide with pr—*Aaaaah!*

He never finished. Not that I heard.
Throont! Throont!

The pirates easily sliced the ropes to the dinghy. There came a creaking and scratching, then only Emily and Daniel's screams filled the air.

I watched helplessly as the dinghy tumbled into the ash and disappeared. My friends' cries for help echoed hauntingly.

"Ready the plank!" Captain Halfhand commanded without a thought to what had just happened. "Let's see this traitor join his friends."

I slumped against the railing, numb inside and out. Five minutes ago, my friends and I had been about to escape. Now they were gone and I was headed for the plank.

Captain Halfhand grabbed my collar and started to drag me across the ship. "On deck, ye lazy curs!" he bellowed, pounding his feet. "On deck!"

Hatches and doorways flew open, and ghoulish crewmen shambled onto the deck. When they spied me with their captain, their eyes flashed cruelly. A prisoner headed for the plank was something to celebrate.

"Give 'im the heave-ho, cap'n," a crewman barked eagerly.

"Off to 'Deep with ye, boy!" another croaked.

When I heard them, I lost hope. *It's over*, I thought bleakly. *This is as bad as it gets.*

Amazingly, I was wrong. It could get worse, and did. I'd forgotten that there are things that are worse than pirates.

Ooowhooo-ooh-ooo.

Two dozen shaddim rose through the fog as lightly as clouds. They glided speedily toward the ship, their eyes more sinister than any pirate's—even a ghoulish pirate's.

Ooowhooo-ooh-ooo.

"What manner 'o foul creature…?" Captain Halfhand gasped.

I almost laughed at his reaction. Foul creatures! Talk about the pot calling the kettle black! Hadn't he looked in a mirror lately?

"Light!" I cried urgently. "We need lots of light, or water. Those are the only things that'll chase the shaddim away."

Captain Halfhand glanced at me. "Shaddim? Ye know these creatures?"

Oops! Now I'd done it. If Halfhand discovered that the shaddim were after me, he would probably toss me over the railing. Plank or no plank.

"They're after Emily," I covered quickly. "The girl that … was with me." I choked on the words. I couldn't bring myself to say *the girl you just killed*. "They must think she's still here."

I'm not sure if Halfhand believed my story, but he wasn't taking chances.

"Light fires!" he roared at his crew. "Or we're all goin' down with the ship!"

Ooowhooo-ooh-ooo.

The shaddim floated nearer, and the pirates struck up torches. There was going to be a war between monsters, and I would be the trophy awarded to the victor.

A Plead to Greed

19

The shaddim struck quickly. Their whip-like arms
snapped to attack. Their moaning choked the air.
Ooowhooo-ooh-ooo.

Halfhand's crewmen scrambled to defend themselves.
Chains and swords flashed. Clubs whistled. Torchlight
blazed and streaked in the darkness.

Still, the anguished cries of the crew pierced the night.
The shaddim were too fast and too fearless. A few torches
couldn't keep them all at bay.

"Form a circle!" Halfhand bellowed, trying to maintain
order. "Keep those torches up high!"

Pirates collapsed into shaddim sleep everywhere I
looked. Some dropped their weapons and clutched invisible wounds. Others toppled over stiffly like statues,
thudding lifelessly onto the deck.

"We can't stay here!" I shouted.

In minutes, the crew would be overrun. There were too
many shaddim, and more kept rising from the ash. There

must have been more than fifty of them.

Ooowhooo-ooh-ooo.

Captain Halfhand glanced angrily at me. "The captain always goes down with his ship, m'boy. Where's your honor?"

I gawked at him. *Honor?* What did he know about honor? He was a monster, more ghoul than pirate. Besides, since when were pirates honorable? All they cared about was—

Treasure! That was it. I could use Captain Halfhand's greed to get him to listen to me.

"The shaddim want this," I told him hurriedly, tapping the Dragonsbane Horn where it was attached to my hip. "They're after me."

Just as I'd hoped, Halfhand gawked at the sight of the Horn. Pirates couldn't resist new treasure.

"What is it?" he demanded. A sparkle gleamed in his jeweled eyes.

"The Dragonsbane Horn," I said in my deepest voice, trying to sound serious and important. "It can control dragons." Then, when I knew I had his attention, I added, "It's worth a fortune."

The gleam in Halfhand's eyes became a meteor. "How much?" he growled, sounding a little like a purring cat. A big, mangy cat.

"Enough to buy—" I started when an ear-splitting shriek

made me cringe.

Before I knew what was happening, a gruesome pirate tumbled into my arms and knocked me to the deck. As stiff as a board, the pirate stared at me with unblinking eyes. His mouth was slack like the loose jawbone on a skull.

I recognized the look. It came from being put to sleep by shaddim.

Disgusted and trying not to shriek myself, I shoved with my arms and heaved with my legs. The pirate slid woodenly off of me, and I squinted up into—

Flaming eyes.

Ooowhooo-ooh-ooo.

A shaddim floated directly above me. Its hollow mouth gaped wide in a chilling moan. Through it, I spotted the pale glow of the full moon.

My shriek exploded in full force.

As if in slow motion, the shaddim drew back its arms to strike, but I couldn't move. I was frozen with terror, and the only sound I heard was the pounding of my own heart.

I squeezed my eyes shut. I couldn't stop the shaddim but I didn't have to watch.

Glizzz-zzk!

Light suddenly flared behind my eyelids, and the shaddim squealed. The sound was different, not a moan. It reminded me of fingernails scraping over a chalkboard.

Then a strong hand missing two fingers grasped my elbow and hauled me to my feet. "Let's go, m'boy," Captain Halfhand barked. "We've got us a fortune to spend."

I blinked, more than a little amazed. "You saved ..." I mumbled. A torch sputtered on the deck near Halfhand's feet.

"C'mon," Halfhand said gruffly, and I nodded quickly. I didn't think he would lead me into a trap. Not so soon after saving me.

That's not to say I trusted him. He was still a ghoul and a pirate. Only his greed for the Horn encouraged him to help me.

More than half of his crew lay motionless on the deck. Fallen torches burned here and there, starting small fires on the deck. The whole ship was threatening to go up in flames.

We raced across the deck, hurdling sleeping pirates and dodging shaddim. Halfhand held a torch in front of him like a sword and slashed at anything that moved.

Ooowhooo-ooh-ooo.

Shaddim moaned in pursuit. Their bat-like wings fluttered noisily like a hundred voices whispering at once. Chilling words echoed dreamily in my ears.

Draaagonsbaaane, Mother wantsss the Horn. Give it to usss.

I grunted in response. "Is that all you can say?" I shouted wildly. I'd heard those words before. "Learn a new song! I'm tired of that one."

The shaddim ignored me and moaned louder.

"In here!" Captain Halfhand roared, throwing open a cabin door. "Hurry!" He nearly bowled me over as he charged through himself and then slammed the door shut.

I collapsed to the floor, gasping for breath. We weren't out of danger yet. Shaddim prowled the air, and growing fires scorched the deck, sails, and masts outside the cabin's windows.

If the fires got any bigger, they might chase the shaddim away. But they would also destroy the ship. Things were going from bad to worse in a hurry.

"What's next?" I asked. "How are we going to escape?"

Halfhand grinned slowly. The look was anything but human. "Give me that Horn," he demanded, the fingers on his half hand twitching.

I climbed to my feet, never taking my eyes from his. The wild look on his face told me something dangerous.

Captain Halfhand didn't fear the shaddim anymore. He wasn't even worried about his burning ship. His only thought was of the Horn.

I've unleashed a monster, I realized, backing away. The pirate's greed couldn't be controlled.

"How are we going to escape?" I repeated weakly, my mouth painfully dry.

Halfhand didn't answer. Instead, he wrapped his three fingers around the door handle.

"Give it to me," he threatened, "or I'll open this door. If I can't have the Horn, I'll let yer friends take it."

As if to back up that threat, shaddim suddenly started to claw and scratch on the door. Dark shapes writhed outside the cabin window. Their eyes reflected the flames all over the ship.

Ooowhooo-ooh-ooo.

I didn't have much of a choice. So I unfastened the Horn from my belt and took a step forward.

Down With the Ship

20

"That's right," Captain Halfhand snarled. "C'mere." I couldn't be sure if he was speaking to me or to the Horn. His eyes never blinked.

I didn't believe for a second that he would rethink his threat. If I didn't give the Horn to him, he would open the door and let the shaddim into the cabin.

My mind worked double-time, thinking furiously. There had to be a way out of this!

But I couldn't fly off the ship, and I didn't know any magic. I didn't even have an efreet bottle like Daniel had. All I had was—

The Horn!

How could I have been so blind? I'd gotten so used to protecting the Horn that I'd forgotten it could protect me, too.

Halfway across the cabin, I stopped and raised the Horn to my lips. I took a deep breath.

"*W*-what are ye doin'?" Halfhand demanded nervously,

starting toward me. I'd finally gotten his attention again.

Too late, I thought, but didn't repeat it out loud. I couldn't waste my breath or delay. I put my lips against the Horn and blew for all I was worth.

Vwarrr-Ooooohnnn!

A tidal wave of sound erupted from the Horn. Glass shattered, wood splintered, and sails split apart, shredded into scraps. Wind tore through the cabin, punching holes in the walls and ripping the door from its hinges. The whole ship was coming apart.

The raging force blasted me off my feet and sent Captain Halfhand sprawling backward. The metal, jewels, and bones of his unnatural body clattered like a sack of dropped stones. For a moment, I blacked out.

When I came to, I found myself lying on my back. My feet and legs were higher than my head, as if I had a pillow under them instead of in the usual spot. Then I started to slide backward and upside down.

What was happening?

I struggled to roll over and catch myself, but my feet continued to rise. Now I felt like I was sledding headfirst down a steep hill.

"*Ungh!*" I grunted as I slid into a table, dragging it down with me. Small pieces of furniture tumbled alongside me. Was this why pirates slept in hammocks?

I crashed into the far wall when there was no room left to

slide. But the ship continued to tip and sag at a dangerous angle. If not for the wall, I would have continued falling.

Suddenly I knew what was happening. The ship was dropping slowly to the ground. The weight of Captain Halfhand's treasure was dragging one side of the ship down faster than the other.

We were going to crash from hundreds of feet in the air!

I struggled to take a peek outside the windows and regretted it immediately. Things had definitely gotten worse.

Most of the ship was on fire. Orange flames licked the masts and tattered sails. Smoke from the fires churned in the air, mixing with the ash over Hollowdeep, now above the ship as it fell.

Only two efreet remained chained to the prow, and the back end of the ship had nothing to keep it afloat. If not for those two efreet, we would have crashed already.

Sweaty fingers clawed at my ankle. "*G*-give me … the Horn," gasped a weak, scratchy voice.

Captain Halfhand had crawled across the cabin floor. His clothing and greasy hair were rumpled, and the gem in one of his eye sockets had shattered, leaving a gaping hole. But the pirate was alive and still driven by greed.

"We can … split the fortune," he croaked. "I have me … a bottle. Let's *t*-trade." He awkwardly pulled an efreet bottle from inside his doublet.

I shook my head and kicked his hand away, more disgusted than ever. I was finished making deals with pirates.

Besides, Halfhand should have offered to help earlier. Sometimes better late than never isn't really any better.

"Save *yerself*," I sneered, imitating his way of talking. He would have to take the Horn by force, and I doubted that he could do it in his current condition.

Still, if there was one extra efreet bottle, maybe there was another. A captain used to cheating death should have a back-up plan. A couple of them, at least.

I heaved myself up, using the table for support.

"*W*-where ye goin'?" Halfhand whined pitifully. "Don't take...me *H*-horn away."

This time I ignored him. I had more important things to worry about. Things like—

A river of boiling lava!

Leaning against the table, I gasped at my first glance over the stern—the back—of the ship. Red lava swirled and bubbled with life directly below. We were headed straight toward it.

"Hang on!" I screamed, knowing it was useless. The lava would devour the ship and everything on it.

I threw myself to the floor and covered my head with my hands. I didn't want to die!

21

S-G-L-O-O-O-S-C-H!

Captain Halfhand's ship splashed into the red river like a whale doing a belly flop. Funnels of red liquid erupted high into the air. Waves crashed over the riverbanks.

For a brief second, I thought I was lucky to be alive. Then I was flying again, tossed from the ship on impact like a loose board.

My arms and legs whirled crazily. My mouth let loose a scream. Where was my good luck now?

Sploonk!

I went under, fighting against the river's current. I was desperate for air and didn't have much time.

I clawed my way to the surface, coughed, then gasped in surprise. The river wasn't lava! I was alive.

To my right, the pirate ship bobbed upriver, sinking fast. It was a bulky shadow in the darkness. There was no sign of Captain Halfhand or his crew. There was no sound of shaddim either.

Why had the water looked like lava? I wondered as I started swimming toward shore. The river was reddish and warm but not lava. It felt like a warm bath.

Wholmph!

An answer came sooner than I'd expected.

Something big bumped my leg. Something hot, slippery, and alive. The temperature of the water warmed as we collided.

I'd never been a great swimmer until then. Practice might make perfect, but so could fear. Exhale, right stroke, left stroke, inhale. My legs could hardly keep up.

Just when I dared to hope I'd reach the riverbank, the monster returned. An eerie crimson glow spread through the water as it approached. Red scales like those on a dragon rose from below.

"Talon!" I shouted, forgetting what had happened to her. I was in trouble and needed help. That's all I knew.

The monster sliced through the surface, taking me with it. I had just enough time to squeeze my eyes shut before being lifted completely out of the water. Straddling it as if it were a tree trunk, I hung on with my arms and legs, and didn't move.

At least I'm not going to drown, I thought, sweating. The monster was burning up.

So were my eyes, for that matter. I could see, or at least *feel,* the creature's crimson glow from behind my eyelids.

107

I peeked them open and winced. Red light blazed all around. It flooded the water and clouded the sky.

Worse, the creature wasn't alone. The river was teeming with crimson serpents, a whole school of them.

The creatures reminded me of flattened, overgrown snakes. Some of them were over ten feet long. All of them glowed like hot—

Lava!

That was what I'd seen from Halfhand's ship. Not lava. Lava serpents. That understanding didn't make me feel much better about my situation.

The riverbanks zoomed past, and the pirate ship shrank rapidly in the distance. I thought I spotted several human-shaped figures swimming to shore, but the strange light made it difficult to be sure.

Soon I lost sight of them, and lumpy hills appeared along the shore. Each one was taller than the last, like people lined up according to height. It seemed we were headed somewhere, but where?

Guh-lup!

Suddenly the river dipped sharply and I was thrown into the water. Scaled bodies surged all around, shoving and slithering recklessly past. I could barely tell which way was up.

Thwarng-g-g!

I slammed into something solid but springy. A cord as

thick as rope dangled into the water like fishing line, but what size fisherman needed line that thick?

In a split second, I decided it didn't matter. I had to get out of the river.

I clutched the cord and started to climb. That's when it jerked upward as if a fisherman were setting his hook and slipped through my hands.

Screaming, I slid down. My hands struggled to regain their grip, but the cord was too slick. It was like trying to get a grip on a greased pole.

Now I'm going to drown, I decided. I'd escaped undead pirates, shaddim, and sludgemites only to be done in by warm water.

Then my backside landed on something solid, and I was hauled upward along with the cord. A curved metal bar with one sharp tip formed a half circle around my thighs.

A fishhook! I realized. I'd been caught by a giant fisherman!

22

"Ho, ho! What do we have here?"

The booming voice came from above, on the other end of the fishing line. It sounded big enough to belong to a giant, and slow enough for a snail. In fact, it sounded downright *muscular*.

I squinted into the darkness. A few boulders lined the steep wall of the river, but I saw nothing else.

"Better hit the rocks, Petoskey, if all you can catch is a minnow," a new voice rumbled, equally big.

"Ho, ho!" thundered yet another voice.

I squinted again. The speakers sounded enormous. Why couldn't I see anyone?

"*H*-hello?" I called timidly.

"What's this?" one of the giants asked, sounding surprised. "Did the minnow say something? Speak up, tiny one."

"Ho, ho!" another laughed. "It's too tiny to be loud."

This was getting ridiculous. My rescuers thought I was a

tiny fish. A tiny talking fish, but a fish.

"I'm not a fish!" I yelled as loudly as I could without losing my balance on the fishhook.

"Hmm," the first giant quaked, the one named Petoskey. "I've never heard of a notafish fish."

This brought more laughter. "Ho, ho! So small we've never heard of it."

I groaned and gave up. The giants were impossibly dense. Maybe when I got to the top of the wall I could explain everything to them face-to-face. Or face-to-knee-cap, depending on how tall they were.

The fishhook, line, and I continued to rise. Soon we reached the top of the wall, and I discovered something amazing.

The giants were living boulders!

"Hold up there, little tom," Petoskey vibrated, reaching out a stony hand to catch me.

Yes, *a hand*. The giants were shaped like blocky ovals and stood twice as tall as they were wide. They had stumpy legs without knees, massive arms, and no heads or necks. Rocky muscles covered their whole bodies.

"*D*-don't hurt *m*-me," I gasped weakly, avoiding Petoskey's slow grasp. I would crumble like an eggshell in her hand.

"Ho, ho, hurt you?" one of the others trembled. "We can barely see you, shrimp!"

111

Shrimp? Now that wasn't polite! I'd always been small for my age, and I'd heard my share of name-calling. But I'd just met these boulder-giants. How rude of them.

"Just who do you think you are?" I demanded, forgetting my fear.

The boulders shrugged, which wasn't easy because they didn't have normal shoulders. "We're mountaintoms, of course," Petoskey answered largely.

I shrugged back. "Mountaintoms?"

The giants—the *mountaintoms*—laughed, sending up clouds of dust. "You don't think hills and mountains come from just anywhere, do you?" they boomed. "They've got to start somewhere."

I stared at them blankly, not catching on. What strange creatures!

Suddenly they rolled into action. They started flexing their huge muscles while posing in a variety of uncomfort-able-looking positions. Their faces wrinkled in concentra-tion, making them look as if they were eating something they'd rather not taste.

"Back double biceps!" Petoskey reverberated.

"Side triceps!" rumbled another.

"Front lat spread!"

"Abs and thighs!"

Their words sounded like nonsense. Were the mountaintoms shouting the names of their poses?

I shook my head, still bewildered. "I ... I don't understand." I hated to offend the mountaintoms. Even with the
name-calling, they were nicer than shaddim and pirate
ghouls.

"Poor little tom," Petoskey quivered. "His brains match
his undeveloped muscles."

This time I didn't bother to be insulted. The
mountaintoms weren't intentionally calling me names.
They were just telling it like it was, from their enormous
point of view.

That's something I'd have to keep in mind, I realized.
Not everyone has the same point of view, and words can
mean different things because of it. To the mountaintoms, I
was puny. But to a grasshopper, I'm huge. It all depends
on where you're coming from.

"Listen up!" Petoskey massively advised. Then she and
the other mountaintoms started singing and dancing. They
stomped their feet, did somersaults, and slapped their hands
against their sides.

   To grow up strong
   The mountain way,
   We lift and press
   Big stones all day.
               We're liftin'.

We start out small,
'Round boulder size,
Before we build
Arms, chest, and thighs.
                    We're buildin'.

    Mountains—You see now how they grow.
    Muscles—Their magic trick you know.
    Mountains—You see now how they grow.
    Muscles—Have magic.
                    Go muscles!

We look like rocks
With arms and feet—
A massive build
That can't be beat.
                    We're massive.

There's no moss here.
We're on a roll
As we pump up
Our muscle goal.
                    We're rollin'.

    Mountains—You see now how they grow.
    Muscles—Their magic trick you know.
    Mountains—You see now how they grow.
    Muscles—Have magic.
                    Go muscles!

More weight and reps
Will do the trick
To bulk our brawn
Up something quick.
    We're bulky.

First rocks then hills
Then mountains tall—
Just watch us grow.
We don't stay small.
    We're growin'.

  Mountains—You see now how they grow.
  Muscles—Their magic trick you know.
  Mountains—You see now how they grow.
  Muscles—Have magic.
     Go muscles!

A cloud of dust hung in the air when the mountaintoms finished their song. Cracks lined the ground where their excited feet had stomped too hard.

The good news was, I finally understood what they were trying to say. Even if I didn't quite believe it.

"Mountaintoms are baby mountains," I said. "The more you exercise, the bigger you get."

"Ho, ho, babies!" one of them guffawed. "You're the only one here who's baby-sized. We're *growing* mountains."

I almost rolled my eyes at that. *Touchy, touchy.* Talk about misunderstanding words! I hadn't meant to call the mountaintoms small.

Petoskey lumbered up to me before I could respond and caught me in a powerful hand. "Come. We'll show you more."

23

"Here we go!" Petoskey boomed. Then she and her friends started to wobble back and forth as if trying to tip themselves over.

"Ho, ho! On the roll again," one of them rumbled in a sing-song sort of way. Then we were off.

Gruntch! Gruntch! Gruntch!

With grinding thumps, the mountaintoms toppled over and rolled heavily top over bottom. I would've called it head over heels, but the mountaintoms didn't have heads, or heels!

One roll turned into two, then more. The mountaintoms kept tumbling and building up speed. Soon we were cruising away from the river.

What a way to travel! Petoskey's arm remained steady, keeping me level while she rolled. The ride was almost as exciting as flying on a dragon's back.

The countryside was a blur. Tall rock formations, ravines, and lumpy hills that looked suspiciously muscular

118

zoomed by. I barely had time to see them before we
passed.

So I gave up trying, and realized that I was exhausted.
I'd hardly slept in days. First there'd been sludgemites and
shaddim in Tiller's Field, then pirates in Skywatch, not to
mention the climb up all those stairs. I closed my eyes for
just a second and fell instantly asleep.

I woke when Petoskey's roll came to a stop. I couldn't
guess how far we'd traveled or for how long, but weak light
filled the air. I assumed it was early morning.

"Is a storm coming?" I wondered, still trying to wake.

Petoskey quaked with laughter. "You must be new to
Hollowdeep. This is a glorious afternoon."

"Wha—?" I muttered. Why would the light be so dim in
the middle of the day?

I glanced up and had my answer. Churning ash hung in
the air, completely blocking the sun and sky. Hollowdeep
was lucky to see any light ever.

"Where does the ash come from?" I wondered out loud.
I couldn't help thinking of Uncle Arick's poem.

Seek your claim from living flame
Where ashes choke the sky.

Petoskey answered quietly. "The ash rises from
Graveboil Crater, a fiery volcano. Stay away from it, little
tom."

The name filled me with dread. *Graveboil Crater.* I also knew without a doubt that it was where I needed to go. Uncle Arick's poem had mentioned lava and ash. I'd find plenty of those near a volcano.

I was about to ask more when Petoskey started moving again, this time walking. We passed between two hills and looked down upon a rocky city built around a third hill.

Square buildings of stacked boulders and thick stone slabs circled the hill. They were gigantic compared to the houses in Tiller's Field but reminded me of something made from a child's wooden blocks.

"Welcome to Benchrock," Petoskey thundered proudly. "Birthplace of mountains."

Muscular mountaintoms rolled and lumbered every-where. Most were exercising in one way or another. Some strained to lift and curl enormous rocks. Others grunted while doing push-ups.

"Don't they get tired?" I gawked.

"Ho, ho!" Petoskey chuckled, shaking free loose bits of debris. "There is time enough for rest when we are grown. Have you ever seen a mountain on the move?"

I thought she was joking until I noticed her squinting at me. It was hard to tell because her rocky eyebrows didn't bend. "*N*-no," I answered.

Petoskey seemed pleased. "Exactly! When we pick a spot and sit among the ranges or hill country, our work is done. Until then, we build our bodies up to size."

I nodded, still amazed. I knew that exercise made a body healthy and strong, but Petoskey was describing something more. Maybe the mountaintoms really were baby—I mean, *growing*—mountains.

From below, the biggest mountaintom I'd seen waved eagerly at us. His voice was so deep that it vibrated my toes in their boots. "Petoskey, come see! We have tiny guests!"

Petoskey waved back. "Hail, Flint!" she shuddered. "Look at what I caught!"

"Ho, ho!" Flint trembled. "I can't see something that small from here."

Here we go again, I thought with a snort. *More short jokes.* But I was curious, too. Who else would be visiting Benchrock at the same time as I was?

With a dusty grunt, Petoskey started down the slope toward her friend.

24

As we thudded down the slope, a voice I never expected to hear again called my name.

"Jasiah!"

I sucked in a sharp breath and squeezed out of Petoskey's grasp. Emily was down there!

She and Leland waddled slowly into view. They looked different but I hardly noticed at first. I was so happy to see them.

When I got closer, I couldn't help noticing. My friends were huge!

I stopped up short, almost tripping in my rush. "What happened to you?" I gasped.

Emily towered over me, taller and wider than most adults. Leland was the size of a small horse.

"*It*-it's this place," Emily murmured, her voice unusually deep. "And the food. Benchrock is making us grow." Gigantic tears rolled down her swollen cheeks.

Suddenly I felt ashamed. The last time I'd seen my

friends, they'd been falling from Captain Halfhand's ship. I should have been happy they were alive, not blabbering about how big they looked.

"*I*-I'm sorry," I apologized. "But we don't have to stay here. I know where we have to go next."

Emily wiped her cheeks. "I'm not sure it'll matter. Talon is too big to fly, and Daniel doesn't want to leave. He keeps calling himself a human mountain."

"A human...!" I cried. "We'll see about that. Where is he?"

Now that I knew my friends were safe, I was worrying about our quest again. We didn't have much time. The shaddim would catch us if we didn't keep moving.

Leland plodded into a nearby house, and Emily and I followed. Inside, Daniel was relaxing on an enormous stone chair with his feet propped on an armrest. Talon lay curled on the floor, asleep.

Like Emily and Leland, Daniel and Talon had grown to at least twice their normal size.

"Ho, ho!" Daniel bellowed, sounding like a mountaintom. "Is that you, Jasiah? You're so small." He popped a round candy into his mouth that crunched loudly when he bit it.

Oh, no, I thought. *This isn't going to be easy.*

I tried the direct approach. "We have to go," I told him, tapping the Horn.

Cru-u-nch! He bit into another round treat. "So soon? Flint says I'll be ready to hit the rocks tomorrow."

Hit the rocks? I'd heard that before. It was what the mountaintoms called exercise.

"*Now*, Daniel," Emily stated, hands on hips.

Skurrrnch!

A tremendous grinding came from the doorway as Flint squeezed into the house. Petoskey tromped in behind him.

"What's this about leaving?" Flint demanded ponderously.

Emily nodded at me, so I answered. There was no reason to hide the truth. "We have to go to Graveboil Crater."

Petoskey frowned, her broad face crunching into position. "I was afraid of that," she rumbled sadly. "You seemed too interested in the volcano."

Flint didn't share her disappointment. "Ho, ho! An adventure! When do we leave?"

That surprised me. I'd barely met Flint. What was his interest in Graveboil Crater?

Petoskey looked surprised, too, and glanced at her friend. The mountaintoms shared something unspoken, then Petoskey nodded. It was more of a quick bow, but I took it for a nod.

"Flint will take you to Graveboil," she trembled softly.

"*Aw!*" Daniel complained, chomping another candy. "I was on my way to human earthquake size!"

What Lurks In Lava

25

We left Benchrock later that afternoon. Petoskey stayed behind, seeming depressed. She didn't laugh *Ho, ho!* once while we readied to leave.

Everyone else in town gathered to see us off. They stopped exercising and cheered for Flint. Some even had tears in their eyes. I got the idea that they never expected to see him again.

That didn't say much about our trip to Graveboil Crater.

Oversized Talon perched awkwardly on my gauntlet, and I sat on top of Flint. The mountaintom tucked Emily and Daniel under his arms, and Leland waddled alongside.

"Muscles have magic!" Flint boomed in farewell. "Keep hitting the rocks!"

Flint didn't roll the way Petoskey had, but made good time. He swayed and bounced from leg to leg, sort of leap-walking at he went. The motion made me queasy.

Darkness came early because of the ash overhead. Soon we were bounding along with only an angry red glow on the horizon to guide us. I knew without asking that I was seeing the fires of Graveboil Crater.

The sight frightened me, and I hoped I was right about Graveboil. A volcano wasn't the kind of place to be making mistakes.

"Hang on, now," Flint cautioned heavily while scooping Leland into his arm. "We have to make a tiny jump."

I glanced down, expecting to see a river with more lava serpents. Instead, a river of real lava bubbled and spat like a witch's cauldron in front of us.

Flint called it a tiny jump, but the river was over twenty feet wide. Was an ocean a tiny puddle, too?

"One ... two!"

That's as far as Flint got. The next thing I knew, we were hurtling through the air.

WHU-BOOMP!

We crashed onto the far side of the river and went sprawling. Dirt, dust, and rocks bounced into the air. The ground must have shaken for miles.

"Ho, ho!" Flint boomed, lying on his back. "I never count to three. Thinking about the jump is scarier than jumping."

I just stared at him, amazed. There was more to him than muscles.

"Hey!" Emily gasped, climbing to her feet. "I'm shrinking."

Daniel gawked at himself. "Me, too! I'm a human beanpole!" he cried. "I need more muscle crunch."

Muscle crunch? That must have been the treat he'd been chomping in Benchrock. Had eating it made him grow?

"Ho, ho!" Flint chortled hugely. "I thought you were looking scrawny. Fear not, I have plenty of mountaintom muscle crunch to share."

He gestured, meaning to give a small sack to Daniel. Small for him, a hefty backpack to us. I quickly intercepted.

"I'll take that," I said. "Daniel has to stay light so he can be sneaky."

Daniel thought about that a moment, trying to decide if I was looking to trick him. "Thanks, Jasiah," he finally mumbled.

"Welcome," I grunted, shouldering the pack.

I'd tricked him, all right. Now he couldn't gobble handfuls of muscle crunch. But I'd tricked myself, too. I had to carry the heavy sack.

—Good work— Talon congratulated me. She and Leland had shrunk to their normal sizes, too.

"Thanks," I thought back. *"We can't have Daniel stomping around like a human mountain when shaddim are near."*

—No. I meant now you have to carry the heavy pack.— With that, she sprang from my arm and into the air.

127

I just smiled.

We walked from there, traveling slowly. Graveboil Crater was close, and the land was becoming more dangerous with every step.

Columns of flame erupted from blackened geysers. Jagged cracks plummeted into darkness. One wrong step and we'd be history.

"This is awful," Emily grumbled, almost singeing her ponytail on a surprise geyser.

"Ho, ho! Just wait until we run into—!" Flint started immensely but was cut short.

Flizzzt!

A tiny creature made completely of flame sprang from a nearby geyser. It hissed like the burning wick on a firecracker and gripped a small, flaming spear in one fiery hand.

I didn't know whether to smile or run. The creature wasn't even as tall as my knee. Talk about puny! It was almost cute.

"Ashlings," Flint growled, pointing at the fiery creature with one massive arm.

Daniel reached for Thornwake, his magic dagger. "*A*-are they dangerous?" he asked.

Flint didn't have time to answer.

Flizzzt! Flizzzt!

More ashlings leaped from geysers and lava all around

us. Soon there were dozens, then hundreds, all taking aim with their flaming spears.

One Last Leap

26

S-s-sklursh!

Daniel's dagger made a watery slurp as he tore it from his sheath. "Watch out!" he shouted, throwing his shoulder into mine.

The warning came an instant too late. Just as Daniel shoved me aside, the ashling's spear found its mark.

Flizzzt!

Fiery pain stabbed into my leg, and I fell to one knee, grasping my right leg. The spear was stuck in my shin!

I cried out and tried to spin away. But everywhere I looked, I saw ashlings. A hundred little beasts chirped and hissed. Ninety-nine spears flickered in the darkness.

"Ho, ho!" Flint roared. "Think again, little pests!" As he shouted, he swung his powerful arms behind his back, then whipped them forward and leaped. I'd never seen a mountaintom move so fast.

G-R-R-R-O-A-W-L-L-L!

The most terrible growl I'd ever heard burst from his

rocky mouth. It vibrated in my ears, my head, my chest, and my bones. It was more terrifying than the ashlings!

"Run, ashlings, run!" Flint snarled hugely. Then for good measure, he slammed his massive fists on the ground like a pair of ogre-sized sledgehammers.

Blamphf! Blamphf!

The ashlings squealed, turned, and fled. They vanished into geysers and made perfect little swan dives into streams of lava.

"They're scared!" Emily cheered.

Me, too! I silently agreed. Even if Talon was listening to that thought, I thought she would understand.

Flint roared at the fleeing ashlings, his hands still balled into fists. The ground at his feet was buckled and cracked like ice on a frozen lake.

"Puny cowards," he rumbled in disappointment. He sounded as if he wanted the fight to continue.

Thankfully he was out of luck. The ashlings were gone, but not the pain in my shin. It stung and I gingerly sat down.

"Are you alright?" Emily asked, bending to take a look at my leg.

The tiny spear fizzled then went out. For a moment it hung there like a charred toothpick before crumbling into ash and blowing away.

"Did you get a wittle boo-boo?" Daniel smirked, talking

baby talk.

I snorted and scooped out a piece of mountaintom muscle crunch to throw at him. Now that the spear had crumbled, I was feeling better.

"That's why they're called ashlings," Flint interjected to prevent an argument. "Whatever they touch turns to ash."

We started toward Graveboil again, walking slowly in single file. Talon circled somewhere overhead, but I couldn't spot her in the thickening ash.

The temperature steadily rose, and sweat dampened our clothes. Smoke filled the air, forcing us to crawl to avoid the worst of it.

Only Flint seemed unaffected. He stayed on his feet, but marched slowly to match our snail's pace.

My mind blanked as we crawled. I quit wondering how far we had to go, and about what to do when we arrived. It was the most tiresome trek of my life.

Hours later, Flint rumbled something that I didn't catch and stopped. My head bumped into his rocky ankle, and I thankfully collapsed.

His stony hand firmly grasped the back of my tunic and set me on my feet. "No time to rest, young tom," he boomed. "We have arrived."

Half as wide as Tiller's Field, Graveboil Crater gaped before us. Lava churned and boiled in its depths, belching sizzling spray into the air. The pit might have gone all the way to the center of the earth.

In the middle of the lava rose a volcano. A steaming mountain of blackened rock, the volcano was shorter than I'd imagined but mostly submerged. There was no way to tell just how tall it really was.

"We have to go *there*?" Daniel croaked dryly.

His question mimicked my thoughts exactly. Graveboil Crater was a horror! Uncle Arick couldn't really expect me to go there. His poem had to mean someplace else.

Only Flint didn't look concerned. "Wait until the lava clears, then go down," he told us.

My head shot up to meet his gaze, and an awful feeling weighed on my stomach. Questions churned in my mind like the lava. Go down into the crater? And worst of all …

"*Y*-you aren't coming with us?"

The mountaintom ground a wink then turned to face Graveboil. "I'm big enough," he quaked. "Ho, ho! It's time for me to take my place."

Before I could ask him for an explanation, Flint pumped his burly arms and jumped into the crater.

27

Emily shrieked, and the rest of us joined in.

"Flint!"

"*Woof!*"

"*Skrawt!*"

"Nooo!"

We must have sounded like a bad day at the circus. All shouts, squawks, and barks.

But our cries didn't stop Flint. He crashed onto the top of the volcano with a mighty thump.

THOOODGH!

His impact sent lava spraying into the air and rocks splashing into the crater. The ground trembled violently, throwing us off our feet.

"He made it!" Emily cheered, pointing.

Flint sat square on the volcano like the lid on a pot. In his slow, stony voice, he chanted.

By rock and stone and muscles grown,
I claim this throne as mine.
My strength and size and mountain guise
Will free the sky's design.

His words boomed as loudly as a raging thundercloud overhead. Rocks cracked and the earth heaved and quaked.

Something awful and wonderful was happening.

My eyes spied it first. *"He*—he's changing!" I cried in awe.

As we watched, Flint's rocky skin darkened to match the color of the volcano. Soon it became difficult to tell where he ended and the volcano began. The two looked as if they'd always been joined.

A single mountain stood in their place. Only an echo reminded us of what had been.

Ho, ho! Goodbye...bye...

It was Flint's farewell, and I hung my head. He had become a mountain, just like he'd said he could. What a way to discover that he'd been telling the truth!

None of us spoke or moved for some time. Even Talon had landed. We gazed silently at the crater and at the mountain that had once been our friend.

—It's time to take his advice— Talon finally suggested.

Still numbed by what had happened, I shook my head. Take what advice? "Flint's gone," I whispered.

Talon fluttered her wings and glided over to look me

straight in the eye. —No, he is not gone. He is changed. Look at what he has done.—

My gaze followed hers back to the crater, and I saw exactly what Flint had accomplished. He hadn't just become a mountain. He'd blocked off the volcano.

No smoke or ash rose into the sky. No lava oozed from the volcano. In fact, the lava in the crater was draining like water let out of a tub.

Flint had single-handedly defeated Graveboil Crater.

I jumped to my feet, astonished and grateful. Flint was a hero! He'd given us a way to explore the crater, and our mission wasn't so hopeless anymore.

"Let's go," I urged the others. "We might not have much time."

We carefully climbed down into the crater. Puddles of lava hissed here and there, and steam wafted up from vents in the ground. The hot ground warmed the bottoms of our feet.

At the bottom of Graveboil Crater, we spotted a glowing red tunnel. It burrowed into the side of the crater, across from the mountain's base.

"Must be the place," Daniel grinned, but his heart wasn't in it. He wanted out of the crater as much as anyone. The lava could return without warning.

So we hurried.

The tunnel was smoky, hot, and slanted downward. It

was more like a chute, really. It opened quickly into a smoky, round cavern filled with many pools. All of them bubbled with lava.

Glur-goop!

A large pool in the center of the cave gurgled and churned as we entered. Something knew we'd arrived.

Daniel drew his dagger and dashed around the pool. He vanished into the shadows on its far side.

Emily unslung Riverwind, her bow, and drew back its glistening string. A watery arrow appeared as if by magic.

I glanced helplessly at my gauntlet, and then at the Horn. Neither was a real weapon. I could blow the Horn, but that would probably bring the ceiling down on our heads. All the gauntlet did was make my arm itch and give Talon a comfy place to land.

—We'll see about that— the wyvern said smugly.

Glur-goop!

I didn't have time to respond.

The lava in the pool belched again, and a crimson shape started to rise from its depths.

"Shoot it, Emi!" Daniel shouted, still out of sight.

—No!— Talon cried.

Too late. Emily let fly her arrow just as I repeated Talon's warning.

With anyone else, I could have hoped for a miss. But this was Emily. She never missed, not even blindfolded.

Her arrow streaked straight toward its target.

Shunning the Gauntlet

28

Emily's arrow sliced through the air, hissing wetly.

In the pool, the fiery shape continued to rise. Fingers appeared, followed by a small hand, all made of lava.

Ssskisss!

Just as Emily's arrow was about to strike, the lava hand twisted sharply and snapped it out of mid-air. The watery missile evaporated instantly.

The hand kept rising and an arm became visible.

"I'm sorry!" Emily cried. "I lost control when I heard Daniel shout."

"That's al—" I started to say. Emily hadn't meant to fire, and the shot hadn't seemed to do any harm.

Talon quickly interrupted. —Tell them to lower their weapons. They are not needed here.—

I squinted at her. *Not needed?* There was a lava monster coming out of the pool. But I trusted Talon. If she told me to shake hands with the monster, I would.

"Put your weapons away," I urged. "Talon says it's safe."

The wyvern responded immediately. —I said nothing of safety.—

This time I didn't repeat what she'd said. There was no reason to frighten my friends further. I was frightened enough for all of us.

The lava creature didn't stop with a hand and arm. It continued to ooze upward, taking the shape of a small human with flaming hair. Black eyes like bricks of coal stared into mine.

"You?" the lava-man hissed, pointing at me.

I stumbled back, gasping for breath. The creature was exactly my size and shape!

Before I caught my breath, the lava-man turned and pointed at Emily. It grew taller, and a flaming ponytail sprouted from its head.

"You?" it repeated.

What was going on here? First the creature had looked like me, now it looked like Emily. Would it copy Leland next?

—Answer— Talon said firmly.

"That's not much help," I shot back silently. *"Answer what?"* Talon still wasn't telling everything she knew.

—Its question. The elemental asked you a question.—

The *elemental?* So that's what the lava-man was called.

I stepped forward just as the elemental began turning again, this time toward Daniel's hiding spot. The creature

139

rapidly switched directions when it spotted me.

Its hand raised and pointed again. "You?"

I nodded, feeling stiff and clumsy. "Yes, *m*-me."

Since Uncle Arick's poem had led us here, I figured the elemental was asking for the Dragonsbane. That meant it was asking for me.

Strange that the creature couldn't identify me itself. I wore the gauntlet. Didn't that show who I was?

"Step forward," the elemental commanded. When it spoke, its open mouth reminded me of the glowing embers of a bonfire.

I inched closer, still wondering. There was more going on than I knew or realized. Things I should have been able to guess but couldn't.

The elemental held out its arm, and I did the same. I was really going to shake hands with it!

Glur-goop!

Our hands met and lava oozed onto my arm. It covered my gauntlet, staining its leather a deep crimson.

"Help!" I howled, fearing I'd be burned. I yanked my hand away with such force that I fell backward.

"Jasiah, your gauntlet!" Emily gasped. She knelt at my side, tenderly cradling my right arm.

The skin on my arm was pink but not burned. My fingers—

Wait—my fingers? And skin? Where was the gauntlet?

I glanced at the elemental and cried out in anger and dismay. I'd been betrayed.

The elemental raised its arm slowly. On its fiery hand, it wore my gauntlet.

Choice and Consequence

29

"Now do you think we should have put our weapons away?" Daniel bellowed, charging out of the shadows.

Emily whipped out her bow. Her eyes blazed with their own fire as she stared at the elemental. "Let's get that thing," she said grimly.

I wanted badly to agree with them. The elemental had stolen my gauntlet. It would be easy to give in to anger and to act without thinking.

But deep inside, I believed in Uncle Arick's poem, and in Talon. I had to trust that we were here for a reason.

"*H*-hold on," I said, still trying to convince myself. "Let's—"

That's as far as I got. The elemental stepped in and ended the fight before it began.

With its arms raised, the creature drew in a mighty breath like a dragon preparing for flight. The cavern went deathly still, and then—

V-v-vrooosh!

Wind shrieked from everywhere, lashing about with smoke and dust. The temperature dropped sharply, and the air burned sharply like ice in my lungs.

"*Wh*-what's happening?" Emily howled, lowering her bow. Her breath puffed out in frosty clouds. The cavern was freezing!

Before our eyes, the elemental swelled larger and larger. Smoke poured into its mouth. Funnels of lava erupted from the pools, splashing into the creature's expanding body.

"Enough!" it roared with a cough like a stoked furnace.

Heat blasted us, driving us to our knees. The elemental was huge now, bigger than Flint had ever been. Its fiery body filled the cavern and was forced to stoop to avoid the ceiling.

"Enough," it repeated. "Your ignorance is suffocating. I doubt that any of you know what it means to wear this gauntlet."

We'd made a mistake, all right, and the elemental was letting us know. Why hadn't we thought before acting? Uncle Arick's poem had led us here. We should have known it wouldn't put us in danger.

Daniel poked me in the ribs. "Tell it your name," he hissed. "I don't think it knows who you are."

Emily nodded in agreement, or she might have trembled. "Hurry," she added.

The elemental had challenged us. Challenged *me*. It

143

didn't believe that I deserved to wear the gauntlet.

I glanced at Talon, but the wyvern had closed her eyes. There would be no help from her this time.

The heat from the elemental's body sucked my breath away. Standing to confront it was one of the hardest things I'd ever done.

"*I*-I'm Jasiah *D*-Dragonsbane," I said shakily. "The gauntlet is *m*-mine."

The elemental's pitch-black eyes fixed on me. They smoldered angrily and were as large as the burners on a wood stove. "The gauntlet belongs to no one. It was not your name that allowed you to wear it."

Right away, I didn't like the sound of that. *Allowed you to wear it.* The words suggested something distant or something lost and long ago. They made me doubt that I would ever wear the gauntlet again.

But the part about my name confused me more. I'd thought being the Dragonsbane entitled me to wear the gauntlet. It was supposed to be mine. Did the elemental still not realize who I was?

I sputtered lamely in protest. "But … but I'm the Dragonsbane."

I knew that the words were a mistake before they left my mouth. How childish they sounded even to me!

"Uh-oh," Daniel muttered.

"Get back," Emily warned.

They knew a dumb thing when they heard it.

"Think you can do better?" I huffed. Being wrong was bad enough. Having it pointed out was annoying.

Daniel flashed his trademark smirk and started to stand, so I swatted him on the head. This was my business. I was the Dragonsbane, even if the elemental didn't believe me yet.

Thinking of that, I decided to prove it. Slowly and softly, I recited Uncle Arick's poem.

Seek your claim from living flame
Where ashes choke the sky.

Speak the name of dragon fame
The lava can't deny.

The elemental listened without reaction, but the words were more meaningful to me than ever before. Here in the elemental's cave, they finally made sense.

Except, why hadn't the elemental returned my gauntlet? I'd spoken my name just like the poem told me to do.

The elemental raised its crackling voice in a new chant.

Dare by deed, not noble breed.
The duty is a choice.

Swear to heed, serve baneful need.
Choose boldly in firm voice.

There was more to the poem! Two extra verses. Why hadn't Wizard Ast told me? And more importantly, what did the new verses mean?

To my surprise, Emily stood and stepped forward.

"I will be the Dragonsbane," she declared. "I accept responsibility."

The cavern exploded with fire.

30

Lava erupted from the elemental's pool, heaving itself toward Emily. She screamed and threw up her arms but couldn't avoid the blast.

Splootch!

Molten crimson and yellow splashed onto her arm, coating her hand and oozing down her wrist. Her scream echoed shrilly, but she fell silently onto her backside, stunned.

"What have you done to her?" Daniel roared, daggers spinning in his hands. He leaped past me and charged the pool.

In his rush, he missed what I saw. Emily wasn't injured. She was wearing my gauntlet on her hand!

Her eyes met mine as she raised the gauntlet uncertainly. She stuttered a plea for help. "*J*-Jasiah?"

The gauntlet—*my gauntlet*—had changed. Foot-long, flaming claws knifed outward from its fingertips. They trailed smoke and ash into the air when Emily moved her hand.

"Don't touch anything," I blurted unnecessarily. "Maybe there's a way to—"

"It's gone!" Daniel shouted, interrupting me. "The elemental. It just … melted, I think."

He was peering into the pool with his back to Emily. The light in the cavern had dimmed, and the temperature had returned to normal. There was no sign of the elemental. The pool was calm.

"*Melted!*" Emily snorted. "You're kidding! It's in here. Didn't you see what happened?" She waved her hand, and the gauntlet's fiery claws *whooshed* through the air.

"You're a human elemental, Emi!" Daniel cried excitedly. "What a weapon! I'll bet you can take on shaddim with that."

I shot him a grumpy look. He was probably right, but that wasn't the point. "Aren't you forgetting something?" I asked him.

Daniel stared blankly at me, but Emily caught on. "*I*-I'm sorry, Jasiah," she stammered. "Here … let me…" She started pulling on the gauntlet, trying to remove it.

That was the whole problem. Emily was wearing the gauntlet, not me. But it was supposed to be mine. I was Jasiah Dragonsbane. The gauntlet was a symbol of who I was.

Or maybe of who I used to be.

"I can't get it off!" Emily wailed, tugging urgently on the gauntlet's straps and buckles. "It won't budge."

I tried not to feel even more disappointed. I'd known she wouldn't be able to remove the gauntlet. Only magic could do that. Once the gauntlet was on, it fit perfectly and stayed put.

"Watch it!" Daniel gasped, flinching backward as the gauntlet's fiery claws came too close to his nose.

"Is there any way to put them out?" Daniel asked from a safe distance. "You know, turn off the claws?"

Emily's green eyes narrowed. "I'm trying," she growled behind clenched teeth. "Do you have any bright ideas, mister human know-it-all?"

Luckily, I had an idea. My friend Connor had been given a magic sword that could change its size and shape. Saying a rhyme turned it from a sword to a lance, or back again. Maybe the gauntlet worked the same way.

"Try saying …" I offered haltingly, thinking as I went, "I don't … want claws. Uh … get off my paws."

Daniel and Emily stared at me as if I'd lost my mind. I didn't say the rhyme had to be any good!

"Just try it," I said a bit defensively.

Emily shrugged and raised the gauntlet. With her eyes closed, she repeated my silly verse.

I don't want claws.
Get off my paws.

Vrrr-rrr-ppp!

With a high-pitched sound like a zipper being pulled quickly, the flaming claws retracted into the gauntlet's fingertips. A faint trail of smoke puffed into the air then vanished. The gauntlet was safe again.

"Amazing!" Daniel hooted. "Do it again, Emi. Make the claws come back out."

That was it. No, "Nice work, Jasiah." No, "Good thinking." Daniel had forgotten all about the rhyme being my idea. He just wanted to see the magic trick again.

Better get used to it, I told myself. Emily wore the gauntlet now. She would be the center of attention.

She concentrated with her eyes closed. When she opened them, she spoke.

Come back, you claws.
I make the laws.

Gwisssh!

Fire sprang from her fingertips like nails pounded through a board. Even though we'd expected it, we all jumped back when it happened.

"Looks like you're the new Dragonsbane," Daniel smirked. He was making a joke, but I thought it was in terrible taste.

I slumped to the ground and stared at the gauntlet.

Glowing crimson lines crisscrossed its surface like fiery veins where the scratches had been. They pulsed softly with magical life.

Emily noticed my expression and sputtered helplessly. "*It*—it was an accident. I didn't mean to take the gauntlet. It just happened."

I nodded without focusing on her face. "I know," I whispered, realizing something horrible.

Without the gauntlet, I was someone else. I wasn't the Dragonsbane anymore. I was just Jasiah, a short, little kid with no business being on an important quest.

I was a nobody. I was an imposter.

I raised my head slowly but still couldn't look Emily in the eye. "Daniel was right," I told her. "You really are the Dragonsbane now."

Saying the words made me want to cry.

31

The bubbling of the lava was the only sound as we sat in the glowing cavern. Too much had happened too fast. None of us knew what to say.

The gauntlet had claws, Emily was the Dragonsbane, and I was …

Lost. I didn't know who I was anymore. I only knew that I wasn't the person I'd thought I was, and that terrified me.

Even with my friends nearby, I felt impossibly alone. They couldn't understand what had happened to me. They couldn't understand what I'd lost.

"Talon?" I called silently. My eyes scanned the cavern but didn't spot her. Maybe she'd flown off during the excitement about the gauntlet.

That wouldn't be too surprising. Talon wasn't a pet. She was my friend and could come and go as she pleased.

Still, I needed her.

"Talon?" I repeated, closing my eyes and concentrating.

I hoped I didn't sound too desperate.

Again there was no response, and I was afraid I knew why. I'd guessed it the first time I'd called. Talon followed the gauntlet. In losing it, I'd lost her also.

I was as alone as I felt.

"Pardon the intrusion."

A polite voice interrupted our silence. Hearing it made me think of a short, grey-haired man who spent his time brewing potions in a cluttered laboratory. Not a wizard exactly but someone just as smart. "I vish to speak with the Dragonsbane."

"Who's there?" I called, squinting into the dark chute that exited the cavern.

My eyes weren't usually fooled by darkness, but I couldn't spot anyone. The shadows looked darker than usual. Had I lost my special vision on top of everything else?

"Show yourself," Daniel challenged, drawing Thornwake.

A small figure padded quietly from the chute. It waddled on four legs and stood almost as high as my knee. Dark brown and black hair covered its body in a thick coat. Grey speckled its chin. A pair of bent spectacles perched crookedly on its nose.

I hadn't seen a creature like it up close before, and certainly not one that big or that talked and wore glasses.

But I recognized it immediately. It was a wolverine.

"*Grrr!*" Leland growled, pouncing forward, but Emily called for him quickly. Leland was brave, but wolverines could be nasty. They packed a lot of punch in their stocky bodies.

Daniel brandished his dagger. "Stay where you are," he warned.

"Dear me!" the wolverine gasped. "I'm not that sort of fellow. Lower your veapon immediately."

Veapon? Did the creature mean *weapon*? The wolverine's speedy accent was tough to follow. Among other things, its *w*'s sounded like *v*'s.

"Who are you, and what do you want?" Emily demanded. She hadn't summoned the gauntlet's claws but held her arm forward as if she gripped a weapon.

"Your veapons … please," the wolverine gasped. "I beg you. Do not … provoke … me. I do not like me vhen I'm angry."

Do not provoke him? Daniel and Emily weren't acting hostile. They were just being cautious.

"Is there something wrong?" I asked the wolverine. "Are you sick?"

Daniel quickly brushed aside my concern. "I'm not putting my *veapon* away until you tell us what you want." He mocked the wolverine's accent. That was a bad idea.

The wolverine's head twitched noticeably, threatening to

knock off its spectacles. "Oh, bother!" it growled. "Not again!" The comments didn't sound as if they were directed at us.

Emily took a step backward. "I think we'd better—"

Grr-r-rouch! The wolverine snarled savagely. Sharp yellow fangs flashed in its mouth, and the hair on the back of it neck stood on end. The spectacles flew from its nose.

"Run!" Daniel finished for Emily.

That was a great idea, but the wolverine blocked our only exit. We were going to have to fight or back farther into the cavern.

"This way!" Emily called, picking a path around the pools of lava.

Good choice, I silently agreed. Fights can't always be avoided, but it's best to know why—and what—you are fighting. We still didn't know what the wolverine wanted.

Unfortunately, the wolverine didn't seem to appreciate Emily's decision. First it paced back and forth across the chute's entrance, snarling and growling. Then it dashed wildly in circles, chasing its stubby tail.

"What's wrong with that crazy thing?" Daniel muttered. We had our backs to the far wall now, but the wolverine hadn't calmed.

"Maybe we should lower our weapons like it asked," I shrugged. "I think we're safe here unless it decides to charge."

155

Daniel scowled but didn't complain as he sheathed Thornwake. Emily told Leland to sit, and then we all held our breath.

The result was amazing. The wolverine relaxed immediately.

"Dear, oh, dear," it murmured, bowing its head. "Please excuse my outburst." With one paw, the creature stroked its grey chin.

The gesture reminded me of the way an elderly man smooths his beard. It also made me smile. If I hadn't known better, I would have guessed the wolverine thought of itself as human.

"I'm Jasiah," I found myself saying, not bothering with my last name. Dragonsbane didn't mean anything special now. That name belonged to Emily. "Who are you?"

The wolverine bowed again. "I am Virgil VonVinchester, advisor to Druid Villow. I have come to escort you to her grove."

"Druid Villow?" Emily asked for all of us. Virgil sounded as if we should know who that was.

The wolverine shook his head. "Druid Villow," he repeated. "*Villow.*"

"Villow?" Emily tried again, slowly.

This time Virgil sighed. "Villow. W-I-L-L-O-W. Villow."

"Oh, *Willow*!" I exclaimed. Virgil's accent had gotten in

the way.

"So, then, your name must really be Wirgil WonWinchester?" Daniel smirked at the wolverine.

Virgil crossed his beady eyes. "Certainly not!"

The rest of us snickered. Even Leland let out a puppy-like yip.

"Bother," Virgil grumbled. "Follow me. I vill lead you to Druid Vil—to the druid." With that, he turned and trotted out of the cavern.

We shrugged then followed. *Vhat* else were we supposed to do *vhen* summoned by a talking *volverine*?

Flooff ... Flooff ...

32

"Careful," Emily hissed, throwing her arm in front of my chest. I froze with one foot in the air, and she bent to pick up Virgil's fallen glasses. They'd been right under my foot.

Now why hadn't I spotted those? Emily's eyes weren't supposed to be better than mine. They weren't even supposed to be as good.

Being plain old Jasiah just kept getting worse!

I stumbled after Virgil, and the darkness gave me more trouble than I'd imagined. If not for the sunlight peeking in at the end of the tunnel, I would have been lost.

When we exited the chute, I froze again. *Sunlight?* We were in Hollowdeep. The sun wasn't ever supposed to show its face.

"How...?" I muttered, squinting at the sky. Patches of sunlight flashed overhead as the ash churned and rolled.

Virgil glanced at me. "Graveboil has been plugged. Its ash vill scatter and Hollowdeep vill see the sun again."

Thanks to Flint, I added silently. The brave mountaintom

had accomplished probably more than he realized. The rest of us would be lucky to be half the hero he was.

Especially me, I thought glumly. *I'll be lucky just to keep up with everyone. I don't have the gauntlet, a weapon, or an identity. Some hero I turned out to be.*

I kept to myself as we plodded across the rocky terrain. Occasional glimpses of the sun did little to improve Hollowdeep's appearance. The canyon was as rugged and endlessly tan as ever.

Virgil led the way, scampering sure-footedly over loose rocks and down steep slopes. His pace rarely slowed, and he seemed to be following some mysterious path that I was unable to spot.

Now and then he called to us as we stumbled along. "This vay!" or "Ve're almost there!"

I'll believe it when I see it, I grumped to myself after hearing such advice for the third time. Hollowdeep never changed, and one boulder looked pretty much like all the rest when you got down to it. Unless you were a mountaintom, I suppose.

After an hour or so of silence, Emily tromped over to match my pace. We trudged with our heads down for a time before she finally spoke.

"I wish I could change what happened," she said, still not looking at me.

"It's all right," I replied quickly. Emily had already

apologized, and there was no point in doing it again. I felt sorry enough for myself. More sympathy wouldn't help.

She stopped and caught my arm. "No, that's not it. I'm sorry, but ... but it had to happen."

I pulled away, trying to hide my scowl. It wasn't necessary for Emily to apologize, but she didn't have to rub it in either.

"Just forget about it," I said. Even to me, my words were a snarl.

"Jasiah, wait! You don't understand."

Oh, I understand, I wanted to scream. *You like wearing the gauntlet and being the Dragonsbane. You like being the hero. Just like I did.*

Instead, I jogged ahead, shouting over my shoulder. "I said forget it."

Not paying attention to where I was going, I blundered into Daniel. He'd stopped and was squinting at the landscape ahead.

"Virgil's gone," he announced.

Emily drew up alongside. "What? What do you mean *gone?*"

Daniel shrugged. "He disappeared just like a human ghost. Right after going over this hill." Daniel stomped his foot several times for emphasis.

We stood at the top of a tall hill exactly like dozens we'd passed during our trek. Dry, cracked earth stretched before

160

us like a bleak, brown sea. Nothing moved on the slope or in the distance.

"I knew we shouldn't have trusted that wolverine," Daniel groaned. "We're lost."

"Not yet," Emily countered. Then she turned to Leland. "Track, boy."

The burly dog lowered his nose and began sniffing the ground. He paced this way and that, then caught the scent of something and started downhill.

"Don't let him get too far ahead," I warned. I didn't trust my eyes anymore, and Leland's tawny fur blended in too well with the rocks of Hollowdeep.

The three of us hurried to keep up. The dog seemed to know where he was going and wasn't taking his time. Dust clouded up around our knees, and rocks skidded under our feet.

In a narrow ravine at the bottom of the hill, Leland stopped. He sat back on his muscled haunches, glanced at Emily, and woofed.

"Track, boy," Emily repeated when we caught up.

Leland glanced at her and woofed again. A puppyish whine followed. It sounded as if he were saying, *I'm done. Where's my doggie biscuit?*

"What's the matter—?" Daniel began, but Emily waved him off.

"This isn't right," she admitted. "Leland never quits

until he finds what he's looking for."

As if in agreement, Leland whined again. He sounded more than a little frustrated.

"But there's nothing here, just more rock," I complained, kicking one.

"Shhh!" Emily hissed suddenly, grasping my elbow with the gauntlet. For a second, I imagined that it was burning me. "Something is coming. Can you hear it?"

I caught my breath, listening. A rhythmic sound like a rowing team working together in precise time drifted in on the usually lifeless air.

Flooff … flooff …

What would make a noise like that?

Emily's grasp on my elbow stiffened. "Jasiah, where's Daniel?"

I spun around, searching, but couldn't spot our friend. He'd disappeared just like Virgil.

Flooff … flooff …

Long Blooming

33

"Look out!" Emily shrieked, yanking so hard on my elbow that I lost my balance and crashed onto the stony ground.

Flooff ... flooff ...

A warm breeze that smelled faintly of roses filled my nostrils and ruffled my hair. Something large was bearing down on me.

I rolled onto my back, legs and arms whirling. A shadow swept over my face, and the rose scent grew stronger.

Flooff ... flooff ...

Gliding through the air came a flock of flat, reddish creatures with whip-like brown tails. They were somewhat oval-shaped and reminded me of overgrown leaves. Stubby spikes circled their bodies like the legs on starfish, and insect antennae sprouted from their heads.

Emily didn't wait. She thrust the gauntlet forward and shouted a short verse.

Gauntlet, help me, come alive!
Sprout out fingers one through five!

Gwisssh! Claws of fire and lava sprang from her fingertips.

The flying creatures changed direction and darted toward
her. Even they knew I wasn't a threat. Emily wore the
gauntlet, and I didn't have a weapon.

We'll see who's a threat! I snarled to myself. *It doesn't
take a weapon to make a stand.*

I shot to my feet, meaning to shove my way to Emily's
side. If there was going to be a fight, I wasn't about to miss
it while lying on the ground.

I didn't get three steps.

Flooff ... flooff ...

The drumming of heavy wings beat in my ears, and a
massive red-brown body blocked my path. I tried to stop
but skidded awkwardly into the creature. Colliding with it
felt like being smacked with an overstuffed pillow, solid
but painless.

The leaf-creature was bigger than I realized. Its supple
body wrapped completely around me, forming a dark
cocoon. The dim light of Hollowdeep faded.

"Emily!" I tried to scream, but no sound came out. The
creature's velvety body had swallowed the light and my
voice.

My world was black, and I drifted in the leaf-creature

cocoon. I was nowhere. I couldn't feel my arms or legs. I couldn't tell if I was breathing. All I knew was the musky scent of roses.

Then light and bright colors filled my eyes. They flashed and whirled dizzily, and I felt as if I'd fallen into a fresh painting of a rainbow.

Leaves of yellow, blue, silver, green, and red flitted above me like a school of excited fish. The clean scent of growing things filled my lungs. Trees of deepest brown like rich chocolate swayed dreamily to the soft piping of flutes.

Trees? My mind reeled. *Where is this place? Have I died?* I squeezed my eyes shut then opened them slowly, but the scenery didn't change. I wasn't in Hollowdeep anymore.

"Velcome to Long Blooming." Virgil the wolverine's accent touched my ears like a whisper carried on the music.

I blinked again and shook my head. That's when I realized I was lying on the ground. A plush carpet of pine needles and moss made a comfortable mattress beneath me.

"Virgil?" This time the voice belonged to Daniel, and I scrambled to his side. He was sitting in the moss, looking as confused as I felt. Nearby, Emily and Leland looked to be in the same shape.

Virgil waddled into view. His fuzzy face smiled. "Allow me to present Druid Villow," he announced.

A gentle rustle like the sound a squirrel makes jumping from branch to branch swept through the trees. Warm air brushed my cheeks, and a woman stepped so gracefully from the trees that I thought she was floating.

The woman was tall, slender, and grey. Wrinkles covered her face and pointed ears, and she leaned on a smooth staff wrapped in leaves. But when she smiled, her emerald eyes sparkled like a child's at a birthday party. It was impossible to tell how old she was.

Almost in a trance, I watched her glide toward me. Where her feet touched the ground, flowers bloomed and shoots of ivy uncurled like the arms of a sleeper waking at dawn.

There was something mysterious about the woman, something magical. Seeing her made me think of a wizard.

"Druid Willow?" I wanted to ask, but a surprise yawn prevented me from speaking. I'd suddenly never felt so sleepy.

The woman smiled her child's smile and raised her arms. The rustling sound came again, then silvery leaves filled the air. They twinkled palely like shavings from a full moon, blanketing Daniel, Emily, Leland, and me.

One by one, we leaned sideways and then toppled over, giving in to the magic of the leaves. I tried to fight what was happening, but my eyelids drooped with impossible weight.

Darkness took me, and the song of the trees echoed in my ears.

Who's Who?

34

I found myself standing in a deep forest. Trees with trunks wide enough for a team of horses to pass through soared up to the sky. Fairies the size of clothespins zipped lightly on butterfly wings.

I'm dreaming, I realized. *This isn't Hollowdeep or Willow's Grove. This is a dream.*

A musical giggle tickled my ears. "Dragonsbane," a girl's voice called, "where has your gauntlet gone?"

I glanced up, eyes searching the trees. The voice had been too big to belong to one of the tiny fairies.

"I can't see you!" I shouted, spinning. Even in a dream, I didn't enjoy being teased.

The giggling increased. "Dragonsbane, where have *you* gone?"

I ground my teeth in frustration. "Come out!" I demanded.

The girl giggled again, and I spun toward the sound. I spotted her sitting on a branch with her legs dangling over the edge. She kicked her bare feet playfully.

The girl wasn't a fairy, but she was not what I expected either. She was younger than me by a few years and had long silver hair. Her large eyes were emerald, not just green, and pointed ears peeked out from her hair.

"Do you like music?" she asked me.

I nodded, speechless. *What kind of crazy dream is this?*

The girl smiled and brought a set of wooden pipes to her lips. But instead of just notes and chords, I heard words in her music.

Ask who.
Ask how.
Ask from this bough.
Your answer is a solemn vow.

Ask you.
Ask soon.
Ask with my tune.
Your struggle is the dragon's boon.

As she played, I closed my eyes and relaxed. The words and music were speaking to me, trying to tell me something important. If I could just listen closely enough …

When I opened my eyes, I was sitting on the branch where the girl had been. She was gone and the forest was empty except for one small figure.

Me.

There were two of me. One in the tree and one standing below. From overhead, I watched myself on the ground.

Which one was the real Jasiah?

Ask who.
Ask how.
Ask from this bough ...

The girl's song repeated. Its words reminded me of hints on a treasure hunt. *You're getting warmer ... warmer ... you're burning up!* But they would have been a lot more help if I'd known what I was looking for.

The Jasiah on the ground spun slowly in confusion. He cocked his head this way and that, paying no attention to me.

How could he not see me? We were the same person, weren't we?

"Who are you?" I whispered, a little annoyed and more than a little afraid. Then even more quietly, I added, "Who am I?"

In response, the Jasiah-on-the-ground raised his arm and waved. My gauntlet was on his hand.

I am the Dragonsbane, he said with my voice. The words were so familiar that they startled me.

I jerked backward, slipped, and started to fall from the branch.

Ring Around Naglamound

35

I woke gasping in darkness, my heart and thoughts racing. *I am the Dragonsbane,* my whole body wanted to shout. I was me again. I was finally me.

Even before sitting up, I raised my right arm. I knew what would be there. What I'd be wearing. The gauntlet was mine.

I am the Dragonsbane!

With my arm halfway to my face, I froze. My arm was bare. There was nothing on it. To my eyes, my arm was as bare as a skeleton's.

I dropped my head and squeezed my eyes shut. *How could I have been so wrong?* Emily wore the gauntlet. She was the Dragonsbane. My dream had been nothing but a lie.

Still, I couldn't stop thinking about it. The music, the silver-haired girl, the gauntlet—all those things had been trying to tell me something. What was it?

Think, Jasiah, think. Figure out the clues. If you aren't

the Dragonsbane again, what did the dream mean?

"Hope can lead us to places ve do not think to go."
Virgil appeared at my side, yellow eyes shining behind his
glasses.

"Huh?" I grunted, surprised at seeing him and at his
words. "Where ... where's Willow?" I hadn't seen her
since she'd used the silver leaves to put us to sleep.

Virgil cleared his throat. "She is resting, but it is time for
you to go. Naglamound avaits."

I cocked my head at him. "Naglamound?" Was that a
person or a place? The wolverine sounded as if I should
know.

"Come, I vill show you." Without waiting for me, he
trotted toward the edge of the grove.

I met him there and looked out at Hollowdeep. We
weren't where we had been before, and the sight made me
weak in the knees. It was as if Long Blooming had taken
up root and shambled off on a stroll.

In a triangular valley below, a ring of flames and lava
cast long, wicked shadows. Jagged rock formations
stabbed up through the earth like broken teeth. A pitted
mound of black rock like a scorched meteor steamed in the
center of the ring.

"Naglamound," Virgil whispered.

My throat dried instantly as if I'd swallowed a handful of
salt. "*H*-how did we get here?" I had many questions.

That was the first to come out.

"Long Blooming never stays in vun place long," Virgil explained. "It is all that grows in Hollowdeep, and Villow must keep it secret and safe."

So the grove really had moved. That explained the change in scenery. But why had it taken us here?

"What's down there?" I almost hated to ask.

Virgil adjusted his spectacles with the back of a paw. If I hadn't known better, I'd have thought he was stalling.

"Shelolth," he admitted at last. "Shelolth and a piece of the Dragonsbane Horn."

This time when my knees weakened, I sat down before I fell. Shelolth had the last piece of the Horn. I'd always suspected it, but knowing was terrifying.

Worse, how were we supposed to defeat her? I'd hoped that we could use the Horn against her. But we couldn't do that without all four pieces.

"Shelolth has been imprisoned in Naglamound for hundreds of years," Virgil explained. "She is not vhat you might think. But she cannot escape and so sends shaddim to do her vicked vork."

The wolverine's words barely registered. I was too afraid to listen closely. Everything was turning out differently than I'd expected. Everything was falling apart.

"Is that where we have to go?" Emily asked, startling me. She, Leland, and Daniel had quietly joined us and were staring down at Naglamound.

I'll never get used to how bad my ears and eyes are now, I thought bitterly at the arrival of my friends. How I missed being the Dragonsbane!

Virgil nodded to Emily. "Your journey is near an end."

Yeah, our *end,* I fretted. Naglamound made the rest of Hollowdeep look like a pleasant place for a family vacation.

"How are we supposed to get across?" Daniel muttered, pointing at the ring of flames.

There was no bridge, and the lava was too wide for us to jump. Swimming was out of the question.

"We need Flint," I whispered, mostly to myself. The mountaintom could have leaped across the ring as easily as a kid jumps rope.

Emily slapped me on the back. "That's it, Jasiah! We need a mountaintom."

With that, she turned on her heels and started back into Long Blooming. "C'mon, I know where to find one."

36

"Catch!" Emily shouted happily, tossing a piece of mountaintom muscle crunch into the air.

Scalp!

Leland watched the candy fall and then expertly snatched it from mid-air in his jaws. In one gulp, he swallowed the candy whole.

The dog was ten-for-ten. Ten throws, ten catches. He was also growing as big as an ogre.

Emily's idea was simple. Feed mountaintom muscle crunch to Leland until he was big enough to carry us across the lava and into Naglamound.

The plan was working, too, and Leland seemed to be enjoying himself. He woofed impatiently between Emily's throws.

"He's a human … er, canine mountaintom," Daniel commented after Leland's latest bark.

Well, *bark* might not be the right word for it. The bigger Leland got, the bigger his barks got. They boomed as loudly as a mountaintom's "Ho, ho!" and threatened to blow us off our feet.

"I think he's ready," Emily said, patting Leland's side. She looked like a toddler standing next to a draft horse.

"*Wauwlf!*" Leland thundered in agreement. His tail wagged, and I had to scramble out of the way to avoid being swatted into next week.

Laughing, Emily asked him to lie down while, and when he did, we climbed onto his back.

Virgil paced anxiously, shaking his head. Occasionally I caught him murmuring dangerous-sounding words and phrases—*shaddim*, *dragon's breath*, *darkness*, and *ribcage*. All of them made me question what we were about to do.

How smart was it for three kids and a dog with a belly full of muscle crunch to walk into Sheloth's lair?

Talon, I need you! I pleaded hopelessly. I tired not to feel disappointed when the wyvern didn't respond.

Clutching handfuls of Leland's fur, we bounded out of Long Blooming. Virgil called after us, but I doubt anyone else heard. The words were meant for me.

"Remember vhat Villow told you."

I wished that I could have asked what he meant. As far as I remembered, Willow hadn't spoken. She'd appeared, put us to sleep, and then I'd had my strange dream. Only the silver-haired girl had spoken …

"Hang on, now!" Emily shouted.

176

To my surprise, we were already in the valley. Mountaintom-sized Leland could cover a lot of ground quickly!

Ahead, the ring of lava loomed closer and closer, a burning barricade like the moat around a castle. I closed my eyes, held my breath, and then we were airborne.

Heat washed over me as if I were standing in front of the snout of a snoring dragon. A tightness spread over my skin like a sunburn. My lungs screamed for air, and even though they were closed, my eyes felt swollen and dry, and too big for their sockets.

Whulmp!

Leland landed with such a jolt that my mouth and eyes popped open. Smoke and ash blurred my vision. Blackened rocks surrounded us like a shadowy army of giants.

Naglamound is the end, the shadows seemed to whisper. *Shelolth waits for you.*

Panting, I shook my head angrily. *Don't listen!* I told myself. *The rocks aren't speaking to you.*

Still the voices teased me, creeping into my ears and knocking on the inside of my skull.

Naglamound is the end. Shelolth waits for you.

"Now what?" I asked rapidly and a bit too forcefully. The whispers had put me into a dark mood.

"Over there," Daniel exclaimed, pointing toward Naglamound.

The smoky, rocky mound rose from the valley floor like a recently covered grave. Shaped like a gardener's spade, it hulked thirty feet into the air. A black crevice on its wide end dared us to enter.

Daniel was the first to climb from Leland's back. "This must be the place," he said, trying to sound at ease. The way he licked his lips told me he was anything but calm.

"Not so fast," Emily cautioned. She glanced at me with an apologetic look. "I … I should go first. I'm wearing the gauntlet."

I quickly looked away, unable to hold her gaze. "Good idea," I mumbled, and it was. Emily shouldn't feel guilty for being the Dragonsbane.

She slid from Leland's back and raised her arm. Slowly she began to chant.

Let's go, gauntlet, it's time to burn.
Show those shaddim they've much to—

She didn't get a chance to finish.
Ooowhooo-ooh-ooo.
Moaning black shapes poured from Naglamound's crevice. Some slithered, some shambled. Some swept out on tattered bat's wings. All of them were shaddim, darker than the darkest nightmare.

Shaddim with horns and hooves moaned with delight. Shaddim the size of mountaintoms bellowed. Shaddim with fangs snapped their jaws, and shaddim with no eyes slashed foot-long claws blindly at anything close.

These were monsters like I'd never seen before. They weren't just ghosts. They were gruesome horrors that looked as if they'd been assembled by a mad scientist from unmatched parts.

Ooowhooo-ooh-ooo.

Daniel threw his back against a rock and drew his daggers. "The gauntlet, Emi! Call its magic!"

Emily hesitated for only a second, glancing from us to the shaddim. The delay was long enough for a new horror to appear.

Arick Shadowmane stalked from the crevice like a hunter. His misty black hair and beard fluttered like strands of spiderweb in the wind. His eyes blazed, and his hands clutched his razor-edged harpoon.

"The end is now!" he roared. "Shelolth waits for you!"

37

That should be me, I cried silently as Emily spun to meet Arick Shadowmane. *I should be the one to face him.*

But the battle belonged to Emily. She held the gauntlet palm-up before her, fingers spread as if they gripped an invisible ball. Her mouth worked, but I couldn't hear her words.

"Asking your friends to fight your battles, nephew?" Arick sneered. His burning gaze bored into mine, and I saw nothing but rage in his eyes.

That was the most terrifying part of what was happening. Not Naglamound, not the rest of the twisted shaddim. The anger in my uncle's eyes made me want to surrender.

Did he remember what an uncle should be? Did he even remember who he was?

Did I? The question struck me like an unexpected slap. The answer stung even more.

Jasiah Dragonsbane. I am Jasiah the Dragonsbane. Gwisssh!

Fire and lava sprang from Emily's hand as the gauntlet came to life. Then she cocked her burning hand behind her and dropped into a crouch. There was no hesitation on her face now.

"I am the Dragonsbane," she snarled at the shaddim Arick. "Worry about me."

She was protecting me, I realized. Protecting us all. Back in the elemental's cave, that's what she had decided to do. She'd chosen to protect us.

I accept responsibility. Those had been her words.

The misshapen shaddim hooted and moaned, surging forward like a tidal wave of pure black. With a single command, Arick froze them where they stood.

"Halt!" he bellowed. Then he rotated toward Emily. I could almost feel the weight of his angry eyes leave me. "So be it, *Dragonsbane*," he spat at Emily. "My war begins with you."

Before Emily could respond, Daniel leaped from behind the rock. "And with me!" he cried, heaving a dagger at Arick.

Throo! His aim was perfect but wasted. The dagger passed blade-first through Arick's misty chest and clattered quietly in the distance. Arick was unharmed.

"Be gone, human gnat," he teased menacingly. "No normal weapon can harm me."

Daniel's shoulders sagged briefly but he didn't retreat. In

his right hand, Thornwake's watery blade lashed back and forth. He had a secret weapon yet.

Still grinning, Arick glided through the ranks of the shaddim. Emily and Daniel matched his pace, shuffling forward with their eyes wide.

This was it, the battle I should have known was coming. Shelolth and her shaddim hadn't turned my uncle into a monster by accident. He'd been a target. Shelolth had wanted him to lead her army.

And the reason for that was obvious. To get to me.

Long ago my uncle had said, *This quest is about you.* Since then, nothing had changed. I remained Jasiah Dragonsbane, even without the gauntlet. The quest was still about me.

Knowing that and recalling Emily's words, I realized that weapons and magic didn't make people special. Those things didn't turn regular people into heroes. Regular people became heroes by the choices they made. Everyone who tried could be a hero.

The lava elemental's poem had explained it all. So had the silver-haired girl's song from my dream. I hadn't understood, but clues were in both of them.

Dare by deed, not noble breed.
The duty is a choice.

Swear to heed, serve baneful need.
Choose boldly in firm voice.

Becoming a hero meant choosing to be one. It had nothing to do with last names or magic. It was all about choosing to accept responsibility.

Emily wore the gauntlet because she'd understood that and had spoken up first. The gauntlet hadn't chosen her. She'd chosen it.

Now it was my time to choose.

"Stop!" I hollered from Leland's back. I wasn't sure what else to say, but I had to do something. Allowing my friends and uncle to destroy themselves was unthinkable.

Emily turned to me first. Her mission was to protect me, and it was always on her mind.

For that she paid a terrible price.

When Emily's eyes met mine, Arick struck. *Skuuu!* His ghostly harpoon flew through the air and stabbed into her shoulder.

Long, painful seconds passed as Emily screamed. Then her eyes rolled into her head and she collapsed like a jellyfish on land. The flames on the gauntlet fizzled and died.

Arick raised his arms in triumph, howling at the ash-filled sky. Like a spider spinning its silk, he formed a new harpoon from shadowy mist in his hands.

"Who's next?" he roared. "Who else will fall to Arick Shadowmane?"

Dragonsbane Again

38

Arick's challenge echoed through the rocky spires of the valley. It thundered above the moaning of the shaddim. It mocked and called to me.

Here goes, I thought, firmly making my choice. *No more wondering and no more doubt.*

"I am the Dragonsbane!"

The words burst from my throat so forcefully that they surprised even me. But I meant them with my heart and mind. I meant them from my soul.

On my hip I wore three pieces of the Dragonsbane Horn. It was time to collect the final piece and rid the world of shaddim and Shelolth.

I was the Dragonsbane and those were my responsibilities. I accepted them.

Before I realized what I was going to do, I jumped from Leland's back. I landed with my arm stretched toward Emily and stared at Arick. Fast words tumbled from my mouth.

Hear me now, I'm Dragonsbane.
Burn for me, end Shelolth's reign.

Feeling confident, I didn't pause. I held my arm straight and waited for the gauntlet. I was the Dragonsbane.

Clink-snick. Trink. Clook. The gauntlet's buckles and straps unfastened from Emily's arm.

Gwisssh! Lava blazed from the gauntlet's fingertips.

Zzz-rooo! Then it leaped up and soared toward me.

Not even when it settled on my arm did I look away from Arick. The gauntlet knew what it was doing, and I wasn't about to jinx it.

So far, everything was working. I was the Dragonsbane and the gauntlet was mine again. All I had to do was get past my uncle, find Shelolth and the last piece of the Horn, and put an end to her evil plans.

Easier said than done, I reminded myself.

—It's about time, Dragon*pain*—

The shock of hearing Talon's metallic voice in my head caused me to stumbled.

"*W*-where have you been?" I sputtered. I was excited, confused, and a little hurt all at the same time.

There was a pause before Talon replied. When she did, her voice was gentle. —You had to figure out the truth for yourself. I'm sorry that I could not aid you.—

The tone of her voice told me more than her words. Talon was heartbroken at having to abandon me. Doing so

185

hadn't been her choice.

"It's al—" I started to say, but Talon interrupted.

—Now is not the time for talk. Be the Dragonsbane.—

I closed the gap between Arick and me. He hunched before me like a snarling animal, passing his wicked harpoon from hand to hand repeatedly, waiting.

Questions and doubts filled my mind as I took the last few steps toward him. *Is any part of that monster still my uncle? Will he really try to kill me? Will I try to do the same to him?*

The answer to the last question told me what I had to do. No, I couldn't hurt my uncle no matter what he looked like. I didn't even want to fight him.

"Wait for my signal," I instructed Talon. There was no time to explain further.

Ooowhooo-ooh-ooo.

Howling like a shaddim, Arick Shadowmane attacked. He was big, fast, and full of anger. I barely had time to defend myself.

Gliz-z-zkk!

I whipped my arm in front of my face, and the gauntlet's claws caught the dark tip of Arick's harpoon. Sparks and ash burst from the contact.

Our weapons locked. Arick's snarling face was inches from mine. His furious eyes squinted.

"Infernal gauntlet," he growled. "It burns my eyes. I'll make you pay, *nephew*, and then I'll take the Horn."

186

I had no response. The monster had been my uncle. What could I say when he wanted me dead?

Arick didn't give me time to wonder. As fast as the snapping jaws of a crocodile, he gripped his weapon in the middle and started swatting at me with both ends.

One touch would be the end of me. It was made of the same vicious stuff as shaddim.

Szzzt! Skhiss! Zrrrt!

The gauntlet blocked his every blow. It wasn't my skill. I'd only held a weapon a few times before. I had almost no idea how to use one.

But I couldn't hold out for long. Arick was pressing in and my arm was getting tired. I was back-pedaling as fast as I could, barely keeping up with his attacks.

Zlurk! The gauntlet flew up to block a shot to my head. *Fsssk!* Another block, this time near my knee.

"You cannot win," Arick snarled. "Surrender and Shelolth will give you incredible power."

This time I knew exactly what to say. "I am the Dragonsbane," I hissed between clenched teeth. Now that I knew what the words meant, I would never give in.

"So be it," Arick scoffed. "Either way, you are finished."

At the same time, my legs buckled and I went down. I landed on my backside, my arms raised defensively. It was a desperate move.

Arick Shadowmane roared in triumph and reared back for a deadly two-handed swing.

Family Feud

39

"Now, Talon!" I cried, desperate for the wyvern to understand. I hadn't had time to explain before, and now it was too late.

Arick Shadowmane stood over me, his dark face twisted in rage. The razor-tipped blade of his harpoon rose and then rapidly started to fall.

In that instant, everything seemed to slow. My heart thumped as if it needed a good winding. My lungs drew in a never-ending breath.

Arick howled and I locked my elbows. The impact of his mighty blow was on its way. I squeezed my eyes shut, too afraid to watch.

Skrawt!

My eyes popped open just as a shining streak slashed between Arick and me. But it wasn't his harpoon. It was Talon in the nick of time.

Distracted in mid-swing, Arick's howl turned into a gasp. I finally caught my breath, and time lurched into a choppy blur like a boulder sent tumbling down a bumpy hill.

Flaring feathers and glimmering wings flashed before my eyes. Wind struck my face. Black shaddim mist hissed as if put to fire.

Terrified, I watched, frozen. It was the most vivid second of my life. Talon sped past and Arick's killing blow just missed, whisking inches from my head.

Sklarngk! His harpoon knifed into the rocky ground next to me, burying itself in a shower of rock.

"Now!" I heard Daniel yell, far away and close at the same time. The sound of his voice got me moving again.

Almost as if watching someone else, I leaned forward and stretched my hand toward Arick. He never saw me. The gauntlet's claws brushed his stomach as gently as a moth lighting on the grass.

Swifff!

That one touch changed everything. Arick's eyes widened and beams of white light streamed from them like the tails of hurtling comets. Rays sprang from his ears and fingertips, too. They bathed him in light, and he slowly fell to the ground.

He's dead! I wailed to myself. *I've killed my uncle.* I buried my face in my hands, ashamed and horrified. What had I done?

Moments passed, long and silent. Then a strong hand gripped my shoulder.

"Rise, Jasiah. Your work is not complete." The voice belonged to my uncle as I remembered him.

I fluttered my eyes open to find Arick kneeling before me. Uncle Arick, not Arick Shadowmane. His long blond hair and beard were covered with soot, but he looked nothing like a shaddim anymore.

"Quickly now," he urged. "Find Sheloth. I will hold back the shaddim."

I nodded mutely, and Arick squeezed my shoulder. A look of pride and gratitude gleamed in his eyes. In an instant he was on his feet and moving.

"You heard him!" Daniel shouted, grabbing me under the armpits and tugging upward. "Quit making like a human toadstool and get up!"

I let him pull me to my feet, then quickly twisted away. "Wait," I shouted. "We can't leave Emily."

She lay on the ground where she'd fallen, and I ran to her. Shaddim tried to block my way, but a thunderous bark from Leland sent them scattering like leaves in a windstorm.

WAUWLF!

The magic of the mountaintom muscle crunch hadn't worn off yet. Leland was still gigantic.

Emily awoke with a touch of the gauntlet. The red veins on its surface pulsed as she opened her eyes.

"Where—?" she mumbled.

Daniel grunted, interrupting. "You two are human snails. Let's move!" Before Emily could reply, he snatched her hands and heaved.

Bunched close together, the three of us shuffled toward Naglamound. The jagged crevice that led into its depths gaped like an open wound.

As we slipped into the darkness, I took a last look over my shoulder. Leland was surrounded by shaddim. On his back rode Uncle Arick, his metal harpoon flashing in the uncommon light of Hollowdeep.

Key In Hand

40

The black of Naglamound swallowed us like a hungry beast. It hung in the air and filled our breath. It clung greedily to our clothes. Even the fiery claws on the gauntlet vanished from sight an arm's length from my chest.

We found ourselves in a wide tunnel, but it could have been a crowded closet. The darkness made it feel that cramped. The chalky scent of old fires was everywhere.

"*Ungh!*" Daniel grunted, tripping and bumping into my back. I turned to catch him as Emily spoke.

"Please slow down, Jasiah," she requested. "Daniel and I can't see a thing."

Her words hinted at what I'd never been able to figure out. Why I could see in the dark. It was because of this place, because of Naglamound. Only a Dragonsbane could locate Shelolth.

"Grab my tunic," I suggested, "and I'll walk slowly." To myself, I added, *I'm not in a hurry to get where we're going.*

Of course that wasn't the right attitude and Talon let me know.

—You're almost done, Dragonsbane. Finish so that we can go home.—

This *was* the end, I realized. The quest for the Horn was really almost over. Soon we would face Shelolth and everything would be decided.

But I couldn't help wondering if it hadn't already been decided. We were three kids and one small wyvern going up against a dragon. We had few weapons and no real plan. Shelolth would likely destroy us as soon as we set foot in her lair.

We were helpless and on a hopeless mission. Gift-wrapping our pieces of the Horn and delivering them to Shelolth on her birthday would have been less painful.

Wings fluttered loudly in my ears as Talon streaked close to my head. I caught a glimpse of ruffled feathers and almost smiled.

—Speak for yourself— the wyvern huffed. —I plan on enjoying *my* next birthday. I've earned it.—

That was just like Talon. She always knew what to say and how to say it. I'd been feeling sorry for myself, but now I found myself wondering how a wyvern spent her birthday.

—Shape up and you just might get an invitation— she teased light-heartedly.

We followed the tunnel down and down, Emily and Daniel clutching my sleeves. Blackened bones, broken bits of metal, tattered pieces of cloth, and something that looked like a crushed skull littered our path. I tried not to wonder whether others had been on a quest here before.

Chilling sounds chattered and moaned in the darkness. Unexplained shrieks and whimpering cries echoed from around corners. Insane laughter hissed in our ears.

The dreadful noises taught me a new meaning of fear. I used to get goosebumps and chills from the average spooky story, like the one about the haunted house on the hill. But those seemed so childish now. Adventure in a world of magic could be more frightening than any tired old ghost story, and a dragon's lair was more terrifying than a haunted house.

Worst of all, a dry voice whispered throughout Naglamound. It chanted slowly, its words becoming louder and clearer with every step we took.

Gather 'round, my children.
Gather 'round, feed strength to me.
Listen close, my shaddim.
Listen close, heed what's to be.

The voice belonged to Shelolth, I knew. Her words were a call to arms.

At last we rounded a sharp corner, and bright light stung our eyes. It appeared as suddenly as a flash of lightning that hung in the air and never vanished.

Streams of lava lined the edges of the passage. They drained from the open jaws of gargoyle statues that lurked upon stone columns at the tunnel's end.

Between the columns stretched a spiked black gate. Seeing it made me imagine the spread wings of some ebon metal monster. A spiderweb of rigid bars formed a barrier between us and whatever lay beyond.

"Time to put that gauntlet to work," Emily told me.

"What…?" I started but let my question hang when I spied what she was pointing at.

Set in the center of the gate was a curious plate with the imprint of a hand. It was positioned right where a lock and keyhole should be.

I glanced from the plate to my gauntlet and back again. There was no question about what I was supposed to do. The gauntlet was the key.

"Ready?" I asked quietly, never taking my eyes from the plate.

Daniel and Emily murmured as they drew their weapons. I took that for a *yes*.

Holding my breath, I raised my arm and placed my right hand into the imprint on the plate.

Churnk!

The plate and my hand turned sharply, and the grinding of heavy bolts clanked and tumbled. Rust and bits of hardened lava flaked from the gate's hinges.

I stepped back as the gate started to open.

DOO-OO-OOM!

41

BLAR-R-RNG!

The deafening crash of a gong tolled from Sheloth's lair as the gate creaked opened. Naglamound trembled with the sound, and lava gurgled over the edges of the streams near our feet.

So much for a sneak attack, I thought. *Everyone knows we're here. Every*thing *knows.*

BLAR-R-RNG! The gong tolled again, rattling my teeth.

"*W*-why are we here?" Daniel stammered, his trademark smirk nowhere to be seen. "I mean ... let's just close the gate. Sheloth can't get out."

For half a second, I was tempted to agree. Nothing was stopping us from leaving and going home. There was no reason to risk our lives, was there? Sheloth would still be trapped if we left.

Emily stepped in quickly. "We must do this. Sheloth is backed into a corner, but she's still dangerous. Just think of all the people she has hurt." Emily turned to me.

"Think of your uncle."

Hearing that, I made up my mind, and so did Daniel. I could see it in his eyes. He wasn't a coward. He just wanted to be sure that what we were doing was right.

It was. Shelolth was a threat and had already harmed many people. We couldn't ignore that.

Daniel and I nodded. "Let's go," he said.

BLAR-R-RNG! The gong blared again. It was time for war.

We passed through the gate and into an underground world that looked much like the one above. Pillars of rock spiraled from floor to ceiling. Swirling streams and pools gurgled with lava.

The one difference was color. Everything in Naglamound was as black as a buried grave.

"Now where?" Daniel whispered, glancing at me. As the Dragonsbane, I was expected to lead.

The problem was, I couldn't decide. The cavern beyond the gate was enormous, and numerous tunnels slithered away into darkness. Not even my eyes could pierce their gloom.

BLAR-R-RNG!

I closed my eyes, concentrating on the sound of the gong. It echoed off rocks and walls, almost seeming to drone from everywhere at once. But eventually my special hearing identified the truth.

"This way," I said, pointing at a tunnel to our right. "She—"

Fear prevented me from speaking Shelolth's name. I felt as if saying it out loud would make the dragon appear. "It's this way."

We crept into the passage, shuffling so slowly that we barely raised our feet to take a step. Shelolth lurked ahead. We didn't want to be seen until we saw her.

DOO-OO-OOM! The gong sounded again, this time more deeply and sinister. Dust and bits of black debris welled up in the tunnel. The ground shuddered beneath our feet.

"I don't like—" Emily started, unable to finish. Her words turned into a terrified shriek.

G-g-Grash!

In an instant, Naglamound collapsed. The ground split like thin ice and then just fell away. We were as helpless as mountain climbers caught in an avalanche. •

Rock shifted and crumbled, tumbling downward. Lava sizzled and spat, spilling into the black depths below.

"It's a trap!" I howled, starting to fall.

But my warning came too late, and there was nothing we could do. Naglamound had swallowed us whole.

42

I fell forever in the blink of an eye. I didn't scream. I couldn't breathe. Sheloth's trap was dragging me to my death.

Memories whirled through my mind, flashing like illustrations on quickly turning pages of a book. They raced from start to finish, showing me where I'd been and what I'd seen.

A crack split along the dragon egg in Sheriff Logan's shed. Agamemnon's fire blazed in the dusky sky. Captain Halfhand's sneer mocked me. Ashes plumed from the impact of Flint landing on Graveboil Crater.

Image after image sped by, and I knew why. I'd heard the stories. My life was passing before my eyes.

That's what happened to people when they died. Their lives passed before their eyes. Now it was happening to me.

Cuh-doodge!

My landing came surprisingly fast. One second I was

weightless, the next crashing onto a pile of rubble that had been the floor above.

Air whooshed from my lungs, and stars winked before my eyes. Darkness crowded my vision, threatening to strangle it.

—Get up!— Talon's tinny voice was an urgent hiss. — Shaddim are near!—

I struggled with her words, trying to understand them. Had Talon died, too? Was that how she could still speak to me?

—Move!—

Almost by instinct, I rolled over and started to slide. The effort was all I could manage.

Kwhooh!

A cold, numbing breeze whisked past my cheek. Black mist trailed in the air.

Shaddim are near? Talon's words were starting to make sense.

I came to a jolting stop at the bottom of the rubble. Dark shapes slithered and shambled down the slope. *Shaddim!* Their hollow mouths gaped as if their jaws were broken and dangling by a thread.

Ooowhooo-ooh-ooo.

Again without thinking, I acted. I thrust the gauntlet before me and screamed a short verse.

Blades of flame, burn from my hand.
Take good aim to leave your brand.

Gwisssh!

Fire and lava erupted from my fingertips, their light
painful in the darkness.

Seeing them, the shaddim froze and fell silent. Light was
their enemy. Then the gong tolled and the monsters
charged.

Dozens of horrors poured down the rubble. Serpent-like
bodies swayed. Jointed limbs creaked and bent oddly.
Claws extended like snakes wiggling out of holes.

These shaddim were like those above, more monstrous
than ever. They howled and roared. They gnashed cracked
teeth. They stampeded like a herd of berserk beasts looking to trample me.

I wanted to run. I wanted to be anyplace else. But deep
inside I found the courage to hold my ground.

I am the Dragonsbane. I am the Dragonsbane. I repeated the words silently, holding on to what they meant.

Becoming the Dragonsbane had been a choice. *My
choice.* But it had also been a promise to see things
through.

As I waited for the shaddim, I realized that heroes didn't
pick when to be brave or when to do what was right. They
were ready at all times. Even when scared. Even when

they could fail.

Heroes kept their promises. All of them. More than anything, that made them heroes.

So when the shaddim came, I was ready.

43

Hissing, chattering, and clacking like insects, the shaddim swarmed me. I'd never seen so many. I thought they would never stop coming.

The gauntlet's claws flared and its magic took over. Up came my arm when the charge hit.

First my arm swung back and forth, chopping as if I held an axe. *Squisss! Vloo!* Next it slashed from side to side. *Quizzt! Sking!*

I had no idea what I was doing. The gauntlet was fighting for my life.

With every swing, shaddim collapsed. Some shriveled and shrank, crumpling like wads of paper. Others puffed into smoke and drifted apart.

Then they started to change.

The shaddim weren't real monsters. They were people and animals that had been transformed by Shelolth's dark magic.

The gauntlet freed them all.

Frightened deer, boars, and horses galloped through the cavern, eyes wide and hooves clattering. All kinds of birds winged here and there. Hedgehogs and bear cubs scurried, looking for places to hide.

For each animal that appeared, I gave thanks. But it was seeing the people that pleased me most.

A young girl in a mud-spattered dress blinked her eyes in surprise. An elderly man shuffled slowly on stiff legs. More people appeared, frightened but free.

"I am the Dragonsbane!" I howled with joy. I was making a difference!

"We know!" Emily cried. "We've heard you before!"

"You're a human ... a human ... You're the Dragonsbane!" For once I'd caught Daniel at a loss for words.

Still battling, I spied my friends on the top of the rubble. They were freeing people and animals, too. Emily rained watery arrows down on the ranks of shaddim. Daniel darted stealthily, stinging with his dagger.

"We're all Dragonsbanes!" I shouted triumphantly, and Daniel and Emily cheered in response. For a moment, we forgot our true enemy.

DOO-OO-OOM! The sudden crash of the gong reminded us.

More rock tumbled down from the ceiling. Shaddim scattered into shadows. People and animals fled shrieking.

The scene was a madhouse.

Beyond the rubble, an immense shadow rose. The darkness in the cavern rushed toward it like water caught in a whirlpool. Shaddim spun, sucked into the air by the whirling current.

"Three little kittens," hissed the shadow as it continued to rise. "But only one wears a mitten."

My friends and I didn't move. We couldn't. Shelolth had arrived, and we were paralyzed with fear.

Thooom!

One of the dragon's massive feet smashed onto the rubble, shredding stone as if it were packed snow. Still none of us moved.

Shelolth lowered her head, bringing it into full view for the first time. Had I been able, I would have fled from the sight.

No scales or flesh covered her body. No muscles clung to her bones. Shelolth was a skeleton of pure and darkest black, a living corpse.

"Does my appearance frighten you?" she rasped.

Thooom! A second skinless foot crashed down, and Shelolth dragged her bones forward. She was dangerously close to Emily and Daniel now.

"*R-r*-run," I managed to croak. The effort made me feel as if I'd strained to lift a mountaintom over my head.

Throoom! Shelolth rumbled closer.

SPENSER

"Yes, my prey, run," she snarled mockingly. "Give me some sport."

As soon as she finished, Daniel and Emily leaped into action as if a spell had broken. But instead of running, they attacked.

What fools! What heroes!

Ffft-thew! Ffft-thew! In a blink Emily launched two shots from Riverwind.

S-s-skew! Daniel sent Thornwake streaking right behind.

Thwitt! Fwett! Thoonk!

All three blows connected, splashing as they sank into Sheloth's skull. I expected victory. Sheloth was finished! But the dragon shrugged off the attacks as if they were pats on the back.

Her violet eyes blazed fiercely. "My turn, little prey," she growled, but my friends didn't give up.

Like a magician who makes coins appear out of thin air, Daniel heaved dagger after dagger at Sheloth. He pulled them from his sleeves, boots, cloak, pockets, and belt.

Emily drew and fired Riverwind in a blur, and her arrows hurtled through the cavern, never missing. Steam clouded around Sheloth's skull from the assault. *Ffft-thew!*

But nothing worked. Nothing stopped the dragon. She was too powerful and too terrible. Her scratchy laughter hung in the air like the sound of a snake's rattle. Then—

Thoom-Slook!

She lashed out one skeletal hand and snatched my friends in a single swipe. Daniel and Emily screamed, dropping their weapons.

The claw came up slowly, and my friends seemed as small as plucked dandelions in its grasp. Then Shelolth exhaled gently as if blowing on a spoonful of hot soup.

Writhing black mist poured from between her jaws. It spilled and spread like ink dumped into water. It surrounded my friends and silenced their screams.

"*Nooo!*" I wailed helplessly, frozen no more. But I couldn't help my friends. They were changing and darkening, turning into shaddim.

An awful quiet filled the cavern, and Shelolth blinked her flaming eyes at me. Violet spots stung my eyes as if I'd stared at the sun too long.

"Now there is but one kitten," she hissed with forceful confidence.

"*NOW RUN!*"

44

RUN … RUN … RUN …

Sheloth's roar boomed throughout the cavern, blasting cracks into the walls. More dirt thundered down from overhead.

As if I don't have enough to worry about, I panicked, scrambling to escape. *Now the ceiling is going to fall on my head.*

First the trap, then the gong, and finally Sheloth's roar. All of them were threatening a cave-in. If that happened, the Dragonsbane Horn would be lost and buried forever.

So would Sheloth. So would I.

Knowing that helped me run faster.

Thooom! Thooom! Sheloth's heavy stride slammed behind me, never slowing or losing ground. She knew her lair better than I. It was only a matter of time before she caught me.

Holding my breath, I squeezed between two boulders and threw my back against the rock. Then I scooted along the edge of one boulder, trying to circle around for a surprise attack.

Searching for a dragon in the dark was terrifying business. Sweat beaded on my forehead. Chills sent spasms up and down my back. I could barely keep the gauntlet steady for all the shaking I was doing.

Shelolth was searching, too.

Grr-Rowrrrerrr!

Plummeting from overhead, she soared into view. Her ragged wings fluttered like the sails on a shipwreck. Her massive claws speared the air.

Roaring, her jaws parted. Bellowing, she exhaled.

G-W-A-U-S-S-S-H!

A funnel of icy black flame spewed from her mouth.

I'm sure I shrieked, but only Shelolth's howl filled my ears. It chugged and hissed and sent me spinning and bouncing like a skipped stone.

DOO-OO-OOM!

I crashed into Shelolth's gong, hammering against it before hitting the ground. If Daniel had been able, he would have called me a human mallet.

I landed bruised and battered, dizzy and close to passing out. But I was me, not a shaddim. I was alive and unchanged.

Thanks to the gauntlet.

When Shelolth's foul breath came close, the gauntlet's fire burned its magic away. Sparks leaped from my hand,

and the scent of burning eggs made my eyes water. But only the wind of Shelolth's attack touched me.

"Ah, you have your own claws, Dragonsbane," Shelolth snarled after landing in front of me. There was a hint of surprise in her voice. "But can yours match mine?"

In that terrifying instant, I almost lost hope. Dragons were the most powerful creatures in the world. What was I doing there?

Dragons were stronger than ogres, faster than swords, wiser than wizards, and more deadly than disease. They could rule all in their sight if they chose, and their eyes saw everything.

Only magic could slow them, and only the Horn could stop them.

Right then, right there, that meant me.

The gauntlet was magic, but not the right kind. It didn't make me strong, and it didn't make me fast. Facing Shelolth as if I were an honorable knight would only get me killed.

Grr-Rowrrrerrr!

With a bellow, Shelolth sprang forward like a striking cobra. Ebon flames sprayed from her mouth, and rock exploded beneath her claws.

This time she was too fast and too close. There would be no outrunning her.

So I did the only thing I could. I raised the gauntlet,

ducked my head, and ran straight at her.

Vlooosh! Her awful breath blasted me. *Chonk!* Her jaws snapped near my head.

How I made it past them, I don't know. Luck or accident. But there I was, still alive and sprinting beneath her black ribcage.

—Forgetting something?— Talon suddenly asked.

"Help me!" I gasped, ignoring her question. Now wasn't the time for riddles or games. Sheloth's bony tail was coming into view. One swat from it could topple a castle.

I had no idea where Talon was, but her voice was steady and loud. —The Horn, Dragonsbane! Use it!—

I stumbled and went skidding across the jagged ground. Talon wanted me to blow the Horn, but that would kill us all. The ceiling was already threatening to collapse. The Horn's blast would bring it down.

—Do you have a better way?— Talon replied, reading my mind.

I didn't, so I kept quiet.

I scrambled out from beneath Sheloth's bulk, turning sharply past her back leg. It would take only a second to blow the Horn. But it would take Sheloth less to catch me. *Thwamp!*

Too late! As I slipped the Horn from my belt, a heavy blow smashed down on my back.

I collapsed in a heap, pinned to the ground beneath Sheloth's claw. Her sharp nails surrounded me like the bars of a prison cell.

"Did you bring me a gift, kitten?" Shelolth purred. "You know the Horn is useless without this."

With her free claw, Shelolth tapped her ribcage. There among the black bones glittered the fourth and final piece of the Dragonsbane Horn.

I'd been right beneath it! How could I have missed seeing it before?

Shelolth lowered her head, and her jaws parted slightly as if she were staring at a warm piece of pie.

"No more running," she hissed, her terrible voice nothing like a purr now. "Give the Horn to me."

Trapped and beaten, I had no choice. There was only one thing I could do.

Won for All

45

Vwarrrrr—

I blew the Horn with every puff of my breath. I blew it with all my strength. I blew and kept blowing until I could blow no more.

—Ooooonn!

At first Shelolth howled in triumph, throwing back her head and blasting the ceiling with dark fire.

"Fool Dragonsbane! Three pieces are powerless against me!"

Then she shrieked when the ceiling gave way.

Rocks the size of my fist fell first, then boulders as wide as Shelolth's skull. They groaned and shuddered and dropped from above in a deadly, crashing shower.

Thash! Blan! Pooom!

But the rocks were not what terrified Shelolth. Her blackened bones could withstand any beating. It was the sun, peeking through cracks above as the ceiling collapsed, that drove her mad. It was light.

As the gaps in the ceiling grew, sunlight filled the cavern. It blazed into the gloom and bathed everything in a golden glow.

Once again, Flint the mountaintom had saved us all. Blocking off the volcano had stopped the ash from filling the sky. That allowed the sun to return to Hollowdeep.

Caught in the light, Shelolth screamed and thrashed as if burned by the strongest acid. Her claws gouged the ground. Her tail swatted the walls and crashed against her gong.

DOO-OO-OOM! DOO-OO-OOM! DOO-OO-OOM!

The gong tolled for Shelolth. It signaled her doom.

—Get down!— Talon cried.

Zigging and zagging through the shower of tumbling rocks, Talon gleamed like a polished jewel, like an armored hero on a gloomy battlefield. She darted to my side and spread her shining wings.

Skrawt! —Get down!—

I threw myself to the floor and curled into a ball. Talon swooped over me and threw her wings around me like an umbrella.

Dudge! Skoon! Flammm!

Rock and dirt continued to fall, pounding the ground with fury. They fell for what seemed like hours, and I trembled with each thunderous crash.

But not a single one touched me. Not one stone or clump of dirt. Beneath Talon, I was as safe as a joey in its

216

mother's pouch.

When the rocks finally quieted, I was still too afraid to move. Then hands grasped my arm and dragged me from the rubble.

Covered with dirt but smiling, Emily and Daniel hauled me to my feet. We hugged more than once and stuttered short, nervous laughter.

We were alive and almost too amazed to appreciate it.

"You're a human Dragonsbane," Daniel smirked at last. It was the first full sentence any of us had spoken in what seemed like ages.

A human Dragonsbane. Was I?

I looked around at the settling dust. I had done nothing alone. Daniel and Emily were the Dragonsbanes. Flint was the Dragonsbane. Talon was—

Talon!

I fell to my knees and tore into the rubble with my bare hands.

"Talon!" I screamed. "Talon, please!" I screamed until my throat burned and dug until my fingers bled.

But there was no sign of the shining, heroic wyvern. She was lost beneath the rubble.

Weeping, I collapsed. My best friend had given her life to save mine.

46

Some time later Daniel pushed an object into my hands. It was curved, smooth, and about as long as my forearm, but I didn't recognize it at first. I was too blinded by grief.

Talon was gone. My Talon! What did I care about anything else?

"Jasiah," Emily whispered softly, "put it with the others. It's the last piece of the Horn."

Numbly I did as she asked. There was no joy in it. No sense of accomplishment. It might as well have been done by someone else.

When the pieces fit together, I expected to hear singing or the victorious blare of trumpets. I'd imagined all sorts of silly things. Instead, the bellow of a dragon shook the ruin of Naglamound.

Grr-RARRRG!

"Shelolth!" I shrieked, horrified. I should have known we couldn't defeat an undead dragon.

A great shadow fell over us, filling the hole above.

Steam and heat blew into the cavern.

"It is time, Dragonsbane," a gigantic voice boomed. "Choose now!"

I glanced up, terrified by what I might see. I couldn't fight anymore. I didn't have the strength. Talon was gone and so was my hope.

Agamemnon, not Shelolth, was the dragon perched on the shattered ledge overhead. His mighty wings blocked the sun and sky.

"Remember, you must choose," he demanded again, flames licking the corners of his mouth.

In my hands I clutched the Dragonsbane Horn. Not pieces of it, the whole thing. With a single blow, I could control Agamemnon. I could make him bow to me, and I was not afraid.

This was my quest, I realized. This was the moment to end it all. I could blow the Horn and become the master of dragons. Or I could …

Or what?

What choices did I have? Agamemnon was waiting. My friends and dozens of frightened people and animals were waiting. I had to decide.

Through my tears, I gazed at the Horn and recalled the first time I'd blown it. I'd been alone and afraid and in need of a friend.

Talon had answered that call. She'd been free to do so,

and had never left my side by choice since.

Did the Horn now give me the right to force Agamemnon to do the same? It gave me the power, without doubt. Did it also give me the right?

I knew the answer immediately. No. Magic didn't give me the right to become a tyrant. Just because I had the power didn't meant I had to use it.

Just because I *could* do it didn't mean I *should*.

Agamemnon was free and should stay that way. Freedom was what we'd fought for against Shelolth. Her shaddim had been slaves, and I refused to make more.

Talon would have agreed.

I took a deep breath, lowered my arms, and then heaved them into the air. Spinning and glinting in the light, the Horn spiraled upward, mine no longer.

Agamemnon watched the Horn rise with an eagle's eye. Up, up it seemed to float until—

Charnk!

The dragon snatched it between his teeth. There came a great screeching and shredding, and then Agamemnon swallowed.

The Horn was gone. Talon was gone. And I wanted to be left alone.

Never Endings

47

Agamemnon stroked his powerful wings, preparing for flight. But before leaping into the sky, he bowed his massive scaled head to me.

"All of dragondom owes you its thanks," he stated, as regally as a king. "I offer mine now. If ever you have need, I will come ... once."

With that, he heaved himself upward and spiraled away into the bright sky. I didn't expect him to speak again, but his voice touched my mind the way Talon's used to do.

—You are Dragonsbane no more. You are Jasiah Dragon*friend*.—

Then the dragon was gone.

"Did you hear that, Jasiah?" Emily gaped. "Agamemnon came right out and said he owed you one. Now I've heard everything!"

She was trying to be upbeat, but I wasn't ready for that. Losing Talon was still too close to my heart, and the debt of one dragon couldn't make up for that. The debt of a thousand couldn't.

We spent the rest of the day and evening climbing out of Naglamound. The broken rocks and sharp stones offered a difficult path.

More than three hundred people joined us on that climb. More than three hundred new friends, people who had been shaddim in Shelolth's lair. People who were now free.

But the one friend left behind never left my thoughts.

Along with Leland, Uncle Arick met us at the top. He congratulated us quietly, knowing our victory had been costly. He also told me he would be ready to listen when I was ready to talk.

I tried to sleep that night but found myself staring at the stars. They hadn't been seen over Hollowdeep in hundreds of years.

"Jasiah?" whispered a soft voice when most of the others were sleeping. "Jasiah, are you avake?"

I recognized the accent right away. It belonged to Virgil.

Rolling onto my side, I spotted the wolverine not five feet from where I lay. Next to him stood a smallish figure wearing a heavy brown cloak. A dark hood hid the person's face.

"Where did—?" I started when the cloaked person stepped forward. She lowered her hood and long silver hair tumbled out.

"Hello again, Jasiah," she smiled at me.

She was the girl from my dream! The one who'd been sitting on the branch and playing the pipes.

How was that possible?

"Who are you?" I gasped, pulling my blanket up around my chin.

The girl smiled again and knelt before me. Silver moonlight reflected in her emerald eyes. "Do I look so different now?"

I stared at her small face, putting the pieces together slowly. Her pointed ears reminded me of someone. The light in her eyes told me I was right.

"Willow," I whispered. "You're Druid Willow."

She nodded. "But I'm not a druid now. They sky has come back to Hollowdeep, and my grove does not need me. It has given back my youth, and I will go home."

Remarkably I knew exactly what she meant. Willow had never really been old. She was a kid, but keeping trees alive in Hollowdeep had aged her. Now that they were healthy, she was young again.

"Take this," she said, handing me a small bundle wrapped in leaves. "A friend of yours gave it to me, but I think you should have it now."

I glanced at the bundle briefly. It was smaller than my hand and very light. When I looked up again, Willow and Virgil were gone.

I slept with the bundle nestled against my chest every

night for a week. All during our long trek back to Tiller's Field. I didn't look inside or tell anyone about it. I didn't want anything bad to happen.

The first night back in Tiller's Field, the townsfolk held a huge feast. My friends Josh and Jozlyn, Connor and Simon, and Emily and Daniel were there. So were Wizard Ast, Sheriff Logan, and my uncle. Even Leland had a place at our table.

The townsfolk cheered for my friends and me. They gave us small gifts, sang songs of our bravery, and danced deep into the night. It was the biggest celebration Tiller's Field had ever seen, but it was not the last.

For me the most excitement came at the end of the night. Townsfolk clacked their forks and spoons on the table and started chanting at me.

"Speech! Speech!"

I stood up nervously, clearing my throat and staring at my feet. There were so many eyes on me, and I'd never felt comfortable speaking in front of a crowd.

"Um, *th*-thank you," I mumbled slowly, and the crowd applauded. After that, I couldn't think of a thing to say.

Surprisingly, I didn't have to.

Crick-tik!

An unexpected cracking sound came from the pouch on my belt. Embarrassed at seeming to have made a rude noise in public, I tried to continue my speech.

"I … uh … I'm …" I fumbled.

Snickers came from the crowd, and I felt my face flush. In fact, I felt hot all over. This was going very badly!

"I am honor—" I tried to start again.

Crick-tik! The cracking noise interrupted a second time, and more laughter broke out among the crowd.

"Dragonsbane, your pants are on fire!" someone chortled.

I frowned, not catching on. I'd just started speaking. Was someone already calling me a liar?

"Jasiah, your pants really are on fire!" Emily shouted, laughing only a little.

I looked down and saw that she was right. Sort of. A tiny wisp of flame flickered on the side of my pouch.

Wizard Ast leaped to his feet. "Ribbit-croak!" he croaked. "Er, never mind-forget that!" Then he wiggled his wrinkled fingers at me and chanted.

We need water-H_2O.
Douse that flicker-flame, now flow!

Glup! Glurp!

The wizard swept his arms over the length of the table, and every mug, stein, and chalice leaped into the air and sped toward me.

I threw my arms up, but the drinks turned sideways in mid-flight and sloshed their chilly contents on me.

Splish! Splush! Splunk!

Their aim wasn't good. Water splashed onto my hair, my face, my chest, and my feet. Fortunately some dripped onto my pouch and put out the fire.

"Now what could …?" I muttered, tugging on the flap of the pouch. I was soaking wet but more worried about what had started the fire.

Inside my pouch was the bundle Willow had given me. Or what was left of the bundle. It was a mix of shredded leaves, ashes, bits of colorful eggshell, and …

Two golden eyes blinked up at me.

… a baby wyvern!

Shouting with excitement, I carefully pulled the infant from the pouch and lay him on my palm. He shivered once, but there was no mistaking him.

He was Talon's son.

He had all of his mother's markings. The same brilliant scales, the same pattern to his magnificent feathers. The only difference was a single large blue feather that stuck up from the middle of his head.

I took one look at that feather and decided. "Plume," I announced to everyone there. "This is Plume. He's Talon's son."

Daniel barked a laugh, the first to respond. "You're a human mother hen!"

I laughed with him a lot, and wanted to cry only a little. I'd lost Talon and she could never be replaced, but I had the next best thing.

Plume, her son. His blue feather named him, but it didn't hurt that he could breathe fire, too. When he grew older, plumes of smoke would puff from his nostrils whenever he snored or was angry.

For years to come, Plume and I shared many adventures, some of them important. The best were secrets between us. But most of all, we taught each other about friendship for a long, long time.

The End

Monsters. Magic. Mystery.

#1: Cauldron Cooker's Night
#2: Skull in the Birdcage
#3: Early Winter's Orb
#4: Voyage to Silvermight
#5: Trek Through Tangleroot
#6: Hunt for Hollowdeep
#7: The Ninespire Experiment
#8: Aware of the Wolf

Visit
www.realheroesread.com
to learn more

Also by David Anthony and Charles David

#1: Alien Ice Cream
#2: Bowling Over Halloween
#3: Cherry Bomb Squad
#4: Digging For Dinos (Spring 2008)

Knightscares Artwork Winners

All three artists will receive a free autographed copy of The Dragonsbane Horn: Hunt for Hollowdeep.

December, age 11
Warren, MI

Nick C, age 11
Redford, MI

Knightscares Artwork
Winners

Clare K, age 8
Adrian, MI

Send Your Drawings to:
Knightscares Artwork
P.O. Box 654
Union Lake, MI   48387

Find out about the Knightscares Fan Art Contest at
www.knightscares.com

Thank you, Artists! Great job!

Hunt for Hollowdeep Artwork

The hand-painted cover art, official Knightscares logo, maps, and interior illustrations were all created by the talented artist Steven Spenser Ledford.

Steven is a free-lance fine and graphic artist from Charleston, SC with nearly 20 years experience. His work includes public and private wall murals, comic book pencil, ink and color, magazine illustrations and cover art, t-shirt designs, sculptures, portraits, painted furniture and more. Most of his work is produced from the tiny rooms of the house he shares with his very patient wife and their two children—Xena (a psychotic tortoise-shell cat) and Emma (a Jack Russell terrier). He welcomes inquiries at PtByNmbrs@aol.com.

Thank you, Steven!